Invasion of the Spirit Snatcners

During the Apocalypse, a group of Mormon survivors in Hurricane, Utah gather in the home of the Relief Society president, telling stories to pass the time as they ration their food storage and await the Second Coming. But this is no ordinary group of Mormons—or perhaps it is. They are the faithful, feminist, gay, apostate, and repentant, all working together to help each other through the darkest days any of them have yet seen.

Praise for Johnny Townsend

In *Invasion of the Spirit Snatchers*, "Townsend, a confident and practiced storyteller, skewers the hypocrisies and eccentricities of his characters with precision and affection. The outlandish framing narrative is the most consistent source of shock and humor, but the stories do much to ground the reader in the world—or former world—of the characters….A funny, charming tale about a group of Mormons facing the end of the world."

Kirkus Reviews

In *Zombies for Jesus*, "Townsend isn't writing satire, but deeply emotional and revealing portraits of people who are, with a few exceptions, quite lovable."

Kel Munger, *Sacramento News and Review*

In *Sex among the Saints,* "Townsend writes with a deadpan wit and a supple, realistic prose that's full of psychological empathy….he takes his protagonists' moral struggles seriously and invests them with real emotional resonance."

Kirkus Reviews

Inferno in the French Quarter: The UpStairs Lounge Fire is "a gripping account of all the horrors that transpired that night, as well as a respectful remembrance of the victims."

Terry Firma, Patheos

Selling the City of Enoch is "sharply intelligent...pleasingly complex...The stories are full of...doubters, but there's no vindictiveness in these pages; the characters continuously poke holes in Mormonism's more extravagant absurdities, but they take very little pleasure in doing so....Many of Townsend's stories...have a provocative edge to them, but this [book] displays a great deal of insight as well...a playful, biting and surprisingly warm collection."

Kirkus Reviews

Gayrabian Nights is "an allegorical tour de force...a hard-core emotional punch."

Gay. Guy. Reading and Friends

In *Dead Mankind Walking*, "Townsend writes in an energetic prose that balances crankiness and humor....A rambunctious volume of short, well-crafted essays..."

Kirkus Reviews

Invasion of the Spirit Snatchers

Johnny Townsend

Contents

The Gathering

"There's someone out front," Nellie hissed, clutching her embroidery tightly. "Kill him, Gavin."

Gavin picked up the rifle leaning in the corner behind the faux ficus tree in the living room. He looked at Nellie sitting on the sofa with her needle poised over a yellow daisy, her flaxen hair in a short bob, both the color and style entirely unnatural for a woman her age. Though he was hardly in a position to talk about what was natural. "Do I really need to kill him?" he asked plaintively. "My record's clean. We can't have that much longer to wait." He was fit enough to fight someone with his hands if he needed to, but he certainly had no desire to do that.

"I want to still be alive when Christ comes back," Nellie said. "We can't allow anyone to kill us or take our food storage and then leave us to die." She inserted the needle into the fabric and pulled the thread through. "Kill him."

Gavin walked to the foyer and put his eye up against the peephole. He couldn't see much, of course. Dusk was approaching and there was a bit of a dust storm outside right now. Hurricane, Utah wasn't the best place to be caught during the Apocalypse, but Nellie had always insisted on keeping a full two-year supply of anything they might possibly need during the Last Days. They were among the few Mormons truly prepared when biological warfare began last week. And when the nuclear bombs exploded across the country two days ago. They honestly had no idea who was behind it all, or the extent of the catastrophe, since cable and internet had been among the first things to go. But they knew enough. It was the End of the World, and the Second Coming couldn't be far off.

Gavin couldn't wait for the Millennium to begin. Maybe then, life would finally be worth living. It certainly hadn't been worth it the first fifty-seven years of his life.

Gavin noticed something moving out in front of the house. In the past few days, he'd heard people running down the street screaming, heard gunshots, a muted explosion or two off in the distance. But no one had attempted to break into their house. Until now. He didn't want to kill anyone, but he had to make Nellie happy. Their only chance of pleasing Heavenly Father was to be successful as a couple.

Killing "someone," though, almost certainly meant killing another Latter-day Saint. Hurricane was a heavily Mormon town.

"Gavin," Nellie ordered from the living room, "do your duty as a priesthood holder."

He sighed and opened the door. Nellie had been expecting this encounter for days. She kept saying, "If the other ward members haven't saved their food storage, they have to face the consequences of their failure to follow the prophets." She was the Relief Society president and continually taught lessons on canning. She wanted those beneath her to survive on their own as well. She was a good woman, Gavin reflected.

There was movement behind the dead rose bush. So many of the plants had withered up and died during the excessive drought of the last few years, and Hurricane had been no paradise even in the best of times. Gavin heard a cry. He raised the rifle to his shoulder.

The crying continued. It sounded like a baby. Dear Lord.

A young woman came out from behind the rose bush carrying a small bundle in her arms. The bundle was crying. "Please," a female voice said. "Please help us. We have nowhere to go. Someone burned down our apartment." She approached hesitantly with the baby.

Gavin kept the rifle pointed toward the woman. The baby was still crying. He'd kill *himself* if he had to listen to that noise very long. He was a patient man in many ways, but the sound of a baby's cry had always unnerved him. It was somehow proof that no matter how good a job you thought you were doing, it wasn't good enough. A message he just couldn't tolerate. Thank the Lord his own children were long grown and moved away so he didn't need to deal with the grandkids very often. Gavin watched the woman slowly approach. She was now ten feet away. He'd be able to make a clean shot. "Go away," he said. "We don't have enough for everyone."

The woman turned her head. "Jon," she said calmly in the direction of the rose bush, "come on."

Gavin was horrified to see a young man emerge from behind the dead roses. How many people were out there? He had to nip this in the bud. Nellie would have a fit.

In the dim light, Gavin could just make out the face of the young man. It was their ward clerk. But he wasn't married. So who was this young woman and baby he was with? Did he have a sordid, secret life, too?

Gavin suddenly felt overwhelmed with sadness. So much sin in such a small town. But they were still alive, so Heavenly Father must like them at least a little. He started to lower his rifle. Perhaps it was best to let God do the judging, he considered. They only had to put up with each other a short while.

The baby was still crying. Such an unpleasant, piercing wail. Twenty minutes with that thing was going to be an eternity.

"Okay, Jon," Gavin said softly. "You can come in. And you can bring your girlfriend and her baby, too."

"I'm not his girlfriend," the woman said.

"We only just met," Jon added, "when she killed the choir director."

"Why did she kill the choir director?" Gavin asked, dumbfounded, his gun lowered all the way to his side now. The young people began walking toward the house again.

"Sister Bates was hungry," Jon said simply. "And she had a knife. Guess she thought I looked good enough to eat."

He *did* look good enough to eat, thought Gavin. The ward clerk was in his mid-twenties, with sandy hair, and so slim Gavin had a hard time resisting grabbing the man's waist whenever he walked by at church. He sighed. Maybe having Jon around would be a good thing. Though he hardly needed any last-minute temptation at this stage in the game. "Come in, all of you, before someone else comes along." He ushered them into the house, locking the door behind them. He directed them to the living room.

Nellie looked at them with one of her sternest gazes, but she didn't question. He was the man of the house, after all. After a moment, she nodded. "I'm Nellie, this is Gavin, we know you, Jon. And you are…?"

"Quinn," said the young woman. She couldn't be more than five foot three, thought Gavin, and she had short, auburn hair, but thank heavens, not in a bob. How in the world had such a tiny thing survived this long? "And this is Harper."

"Uh-huh." Nellie sighed. "Very well. Come along with me, Quinn. I'll show you where we keep the formula and baby food."

"You have formula?" asked Quinn. "But you're so…" She was looking at Gavin, who suddenly felt conspicuous. He had one dark circle of hair on an otherwise gray head, as though someone had touched his scalp with a paint brush. The dark spot only emphasized his age.

"Old?" Nellie raised an eyebrow. "When we were saving our Year's Supply, we didn't know if any of our kids or grandkids would be visiting when disaster struck. We have plenty of diapers, too."

"Thank God."

Nellie gave her a look.

"Sorry. I mean, thank goodness." The three of them left the living room. Gavin put the gun back behind the ficus.

Gavin motioned for Jon to sit on the sofa. He did so, peering with mild curiosity at the runner Nellie had been working on, left in a neat tumble on the coffee table. "You guys just going to sew and knit until Jesus comes back?"

Gavin shrugged, sitting in his favorite recliner.

Jon looked at the one short bookcase against the wall, two long shelves of books along the floor, the top of the bookcase covered with another embroidered runner. There was a small figurine of a woman playing with two children in the center. On the near end of the bookcase was a ceramic figure of the Nauvoo temple, the original one. On the far end was a miniature replica of the gold plates, fashioned out of gold aluminum. Gavin watched as Jon made a mental assessment of his surroundings. "You're in safe hands," he said.

"I could tell by the gun."

They heard a couple of gunshots in the distance, followed by some screaming and another gunshot. "How long do you think we can hold out?" Jon asked.

"We have a full two-year supply," Gavin answered, "which we only just started eating. We had enough fresh food in the house to last most of the past several days. There's no electricity, but we still have gas and water, so that's good." Nellie had lit three candles just half an hour ago, it already growing dark in the house. He looked at Jon's face in the flickering glow. Such a handsome man.

Stop it, Gavin told himself. He wanted to see Jesus. He'd been waiting for the Second Coming his entire life. His Patriarchal Blessing promised he'd be alive to witness the event. If he was obedient and faithful.

Nellie, Quinn, and Harper came back into the room. Harper was quiet now, sucking on a bottle. Nellie sat beside Jon and picked up her embroidery. Quinn sat in a rocking chair. There was silence in the room for the next several minutes, everyone staring at Nellie as she pushed and pulled her needle through the fabric. Jon walked over to the bookcase and knelt beside it.

"You've got to be kidding me," he said. "All you have is books written by the General Authorities."

"What else would we read?" Nellie asked tightly.

Jon looked at Gavin with sympathy, and Gavin's heart melted. What he wouldn't give to hold that man in his arms. Not sin. Just hold him.

"We'll go crazy if all we can do is read books by Boyd K. Packer and watch you embroider."

"No one's keeping you here," said Nellie calmly.

Suddenly, there was a loud bang on the front door. Everyone jumped. The abrupt noise was quickly followed by several other loud bangs. Gavin picked up his rifle and headed for the foyer. "Who is it?" Gavin demanded.

"It's Sister Bowman," said a female voice. "Emma."

The Beehive instructor from their ward. Why was everyone showing up today? "What do you want?"

"Are you out of your mind?" Emma returned. "Half the town is on fire. Bishop Hanson just killed Eric when we asked him to let us in. Are you going to kill me, too?"

Eric was in the Elders Quorum, Gavin knew. Kind of a bum, and not very attractive. Emma could've done better. "What about your kids?"

There was a pause. "They both died from the plague, along with most of our block. Eric and I never got sick, though. It's safe to let me in."

As far as Gavin knew, his own three kids and their families were still okay, spread in cities across the country. No one had gotten sick before communication had stopped, but he knew people all around the world were dying. There was no way to know at this point if it was all going to take place in just a few days, or if the disease would continue until Christ came back. Fortunately, they were too far away from any of the nuclear bombs to worry much about radiation. Of course, who knew what other new horrors had been unleashed on the world since the internet went down?

"Anyone else out there with you?"

"It's just me, Brother Askew," she said. There was a pause. "Promise."

Gavin unlocked the door and let Emma in. She looked awful, her blouse torn and dirty, her mousy brown hair disheveled. She gave him a kiss on the cheek, and he closed the door before leading Emma to the living room. Nellie closed her eyes in resignation. Quinn handed the baby to Jon and pointed down the hall. "I know where the bathroom is," she said. "I'll help you get cleaned up."

Fifteen minutes later, they were all sitting in the living room again, watching Nellie embroider. Quinn had also brought several towels and formed a cushion on which she lay her sleeping baby. No one seemed to want to talk about the attack, or about anything else. But there was a pregnancy to the air, as if the room were about to burst forth with *something*.

Emma looked as if she wanted to curl up into a ball. Quinn kept checking her baby to make sure she was still breathing. Gavin kept his eyes on Jon, so attractive in this light, despite his agitation. Gavin could hear the ticking of the wind-up clock on the end table as the minutes dragged by. Jon kept staring at it, then at the bookcase, then at Nellie embroidering, then at Emma hugging herself, and then at the clock again. Finally, he stood.

"Since it's a sin to commit suicide," he said, "I have a suggestion."

Everyone turned to look at him.

"We can't watch TV, can't listen to music, certainly don't have any books to read." He shook his head. "Let's tell each other stories to pass the time. Mormon stories."

"Stories?" asked Quinn.

"To give us strength to hold out. Hopefully, we'll only have to hang on for a few more days." He suddenly looked very gloomy. "We can only pray that this is the actual end, and not just the beginning of the end." He turned to Gavin. "But no matter what happens, Brother Askew, make sure you save at least one bullet for me."

"You're behaving quite like a child," said Nellie, fingering a flower stem she'd just completed.

"Do you have anything against us telling stories?" Gavin asked. He wanted to do whatever he needed to do to make Jon feel better. And God knew he was bored sitting here with Nellie. Of course, that had been true for some years now.

"Do what you want," she replied, not even looking up.

"Okay then," said Jon, clapping his hands together. "We'll each tell a story, just go around the room. Everyone gets a turn. And then we'll go around again."

"And *that* won't drive us all mad, too?' asked Quinn. The baby had murmured in her sleep but didn't wake up. Still, the sound seemed to comfort her mother.

"It's either that or sing hymns," Jon replied. The look on Quinn's face told Gavin that Jon had won the point.

"Then I'll go first," she said. She leaned back in the rocker, thought for a moment, and began.

The New House

"They're painting today," said Gordon. "Lavender for the bedroom, just like you wanted." He smiled at Monica and she nodded politely in return. He was trying, she could see. It was a start. Once they were in the new house, Monica would put her foot down. Either he'd repent and start behaving the way a responsible priesthood holder should, or she'd go to the bishop and demand a divorce.

A temple divorce, so she'd be free to marry another man who would take her to the Celestial Kingdom. Not someone who harbored the kind of deep secrets Gordon had.

Well, they were secret no more. How could Monica have lived with this man for sixteen years and not realize his true nature? Of course, the idea of starting all over with someone else, and perhaps sixteen more years being wasted before she discovered the truth about the next man, just made her feel tired. She thought about the exercise room being finished in the new house, and the treadmill Gordon was going to buy for her.

She took a vanilla Oreo out of the beehive-shaped cookie jar.

Monica could hardly wait to start packing. She bit into the cookie and smiled. She and Gordon would be moving into the new house next weekend. Only nine days away. Life was finally going to be good. A new, big house in a good neighborhood. It was proof that Heavenly Father approved of her.

"You hungry?" asked Gordon. "Would you like me to get dinner?" There was a solicitous look in his eyes. "You like that new Chinese place. I could get take-out."

It had been years since Monica had eaten in a restaurant, so take-out was always a treat. She was already heavy when she met Gordon, and most of their dates for the next year had been at restaurants, where they wouldn't be tempted to do anything immoral. She'd gained ten pounds that year, but he'd still married her. She was thirty-three by then and ready for children, but Gordon already had four, all living with his ex-wife, and all of them turned against him. He didn't want either the pain or the hassle of raising any more. Monica's doctor had advised against pregnancy in any event, because of her weight. It had been a blow, but she and Gordon had all of eternity to procreate. They had world after world to populate.

"Chinese sounds good," said Monica. "But just chicken and vegetables for me. No noodles or any carbs." She swallowed the last of her cookie.

"Eat what makes you happy. Life is short. Man is that he might have joy."

Monica frowned. She had caught Gordon doing what made him happy. She knew now that confusing happiness with joy would not lead to godhood. "Chicken and vegetables will give me joy."

Gordon kissed her on the cheek and left. Monica listened to the car drive away and thought about noodles.

No. She shook her head and walked away from the cookie jar. She'd just been hired to work at Apocalypse Now, a company that sold food storage to Latter-day Saints here in Provo. She hated the idea of no longer being the homemaker God wanted her to be, but she needed to raise $29,000 for bypass surgery. Monica had continued to gain weight every year of her marriage. She now weighed a horrifying 395 pounds. The surgery was risky, but so was weighing three times what a normal woman weighed.

Monica's first day at work had been Monday, and one of her first customers had confided, "I'm always afraid that once the calamities of the Last Days begin, someone is going to come in and steal my food storage. It almost seems like a waste of money." Monica had started to explain ways to circumvent that problem when the woman interrupted her and added, "But I see you've decided to keep your year's supply with you at all times." Oddly enough, the woman hadn't seemed to say it out of meanness. Monica had so much insulation in her face that she rarely blushed anymore.

But it was still absolutely mortifying to go out in public. Even when she bought oranges at the grocery, she knew everyone was thinking, "You must buy your Ho Hos online so no one sees."

Which was actually what she did.

But she had a job now. She could leave Gordon if she had to, if he didn't repent. She was going to lose weight during the year it would take to save up money for the surgery. And then she'd lose even more.

She couldn't wait to move to the new house.

She wanted another cookie but made herself drink a glass of water. Then she went to Gordon's office and logged onto Facebook. Five of her friends had posted the latest photos of their babies or children. One posted a photo of her cat. Another of her dog. One posted an article about the First Presidency condemning the Boy Scouts for allowing gay leaders. But Monica didn't like political posts. She scrolled on.

A photo of a flower. A photo of a hummingbird. A photo of Jesus. Well, a painting, anyway.

No one was saying anything worth replying to, and Monica was just about to log out when she saw another political post. "Someone finally found a job for Al Sharpton! Driving Miss Crazy!" The photo showed Sharpton as a chauffeur with a deranged Hillary Clinton in the back seat. Monica giggled and clicked "Share."

It wasn't as if she were racist, after all. Her best friend was black.

She wondered how Wanda was these days.

She scrolled a moment longer, but it was all pretty boring. Nothing particularly interesting ever seemed to happen to any of her friends. Monica supposed that must have been the experience of the Nephites after Christ's visit to America, when no one ever did anything bad to anyone and life went along blissfully day to day. That had to be better than the drama she was facing.

If stress was eating her up, why didn't it actually eat her? Take some chunks of fat away? Make the pain worthwhile. Instead, stress always seemed to make her heavier.

Of course, even before her discovery, she'd been steadily gaining weight.

Heavenly Father always gave trials to those he loved.

Monica heard the car pulling back into the driveway and headed to the kitchen. Gordon came in and placed the containers of Chinese food on the table. Monica poured them each a glass of Diet Sprite, and then Gordon offered a blessing on the food. "Please bless the hands that prepared this," he said as usual before concluding.

"Are you blessing the fast food workers now?" Monica asked, laughing. She was going to make an effort to be pleasant. She grabbed her fork and stabbed a piece of chicken.

Gordon shrugged. "Mormons are here to bless everyone."

Monica had to concede the point and ate a carrot slice. It needed to be cooked longer.

"In fact," Gordon went on, "that very topic came up at work today."

Monica knew that one of his coworkers was in a ward bishopric. Another was Elders Quorum president. They were in Utah County, after all.

"We were talking about our favorite key chains," Gordon continued. "One guy said he liked the flashlight on his. Another guy said he had a Swiss knife on his ring. And another guy said he liked unlocking his car from ten feet away with his, and setting the alarm." He looked at Monica with a perplexed expression. "I said I liked having a vial of consecrated oil on my key chain so I would always be ready to bless anyone in need." He took a sip of his Sprite.

Monica stopped eating. She knew she should feel grateful to have a righteous husband, but it was so hard to see him as righteous after what she'd discovered. It was almost like looking at the devil trying to appear as an angel of light.

She wondered if she should try shaking his hand.

And talking of consecrated oil only made her remember what had happened to her father. He'd keeled over in their kitchen from a heart attack. Her younger brother Damien had still been at home but had been no help. He started CPR while their mother called 911. But Damien had just been kicked out of BYU for saying he no longer had a testimony and refusing to attend his student ward. He hadn't actually broken any of the morality rules, as far as Monica knew, but he'd clearly lost the Spirit.

And he refused to use his priesthood, which he still held, to raise their father from the dead. He pretended it was because he no longer believed, but once you knew the Church was true, you always knew. Not bringing their father back to life was simply unforgiveable.

Monica had married Gordon not long before, and she could never quite forgive him, either, for taking her away from home so that she missed being with her father as he passed over to the Spirit World. But she always tried to follow the Lord's example, and she'd eventually forgiven both of them. The attack on the Twin Towers happened a few months later, and that's when it all became clear. Heavenly Father simply needed Monica's father on the Other Side to help the other spirits deal with the tragedy.

Still, Damien and Gordon didn't know that. They should have behaved better.

Gordon, apparently, had been misbehaving for sixteen years, from the very beginning. Monica watched him eat a piece of broccoli and wanted to stab him with her fork. She finished her container, wishing she had some noodles.

She was going to lose weight. She was going to be beautiful. And she was going to marry a righteous man.

"I have something for you," Gordon said with a sly smile. He reached into his pocket and pulled out two fortune cookies in clear plastic. He set one down in front of her.

"I don't want any cookies."

"It's only five calories," said Gordon. "And it's fun. What does your fortune say?" He tore open his wrapper and cracked his cookie in two. "Mine says, 'You will soon find love.'" He laughed. "I've already found love." He reached over and squeezed Monica's hand.

Gordon weighed all of a hundred and sixty pounds. It was repulsive that he could eat anything he wanted and never gain weight. Monica wondered if he had a painting in the attic getting fat.

"Open yours, honey."

Monica broke open her cookie and read. "Confucius say 'Be kind to those who stumble.'" She tossed her slip of paper on the table and put half of the cookie in her mouth, crunching loudly. "Confucius was a false prophet," she mumbled. She finished the second half of her cookie and stared at the empty wrapper in her hand.

Gordon cleared the table and then sat down on the sofa in the living room. "*Family Feud* is on the Game Show Network," he said invitingly.

"I'm not in the mood."

"You want to take a walk or something?"

"Are you telling me I'm fat?"

There was a heavy silence in the air.

"Honey, you're still upset about what happened." Gordon sighed. "We have to talk about it." He patted the sofa seat beside him.

"I don't want to talk about sin. You were sinning! You were breaking our marriage vows! How could you do such a thing? I just don't understand." She so desperately wanted an Oreo but couldn't allow herself to eat something so frivolous in front of her husband. She thought about her secret stashes of Ho Hos and just wished Gordon would go to bed and leave her alone.

"Monica, there isn't a grown man alive who doesn't masturbate once in a while."

"I don't want to talk about it!"

"Every teenage boy masturbates. Every unmarried man masturbates. Every husband masturbates."

"Stop it!"

"Even the bishop masturbates. At least once in a while. The stake president, too. It doesn't make them sex addicts. Your father—"

"My father is in heaven!"

Gordon stood up and walked calmly to the kitchen. He put his hand on Monica's arm, with a look on his face that she couldn't read. "And your father will end up resurrected one day." He paused. "But how do you think all those men in the Telestial and Terrestrial Kingdoms are going to cope with their perfect testosterone levels for all eternity?"

Monica looked at him in horror. She'd never thought about it. A righteous person didn't dwell on the subject of sin. But clearly there would be some kind of chemical castration in the lower degrees of heaven. Or spiritual castration of some sort. There had to be commandments even in the Telestial Kingdom.

"You're going to Outer Darkness with Satan!" she said. "There will certainly be masturbation *there*!" She bit her lip for saying the repulsive word. She deserved better than this. The scriptures proclaimed her price was above rubies. Mary hadn't had to put up with this. Neither had Eve. Or even Eliza R. Snow, for that matter.

"Monica, I only beat off maybe once a month, if that. Sometimes, a guy just has to take care of things himself." He paused again. "It's no sin for a woman to do it, either."

"Our bodies are temples!"

"Even temples have bathrooms."

Monica's mouth fell open. "And what is *that* supposed to mean?"

He shrugged. "Do you really plan to go for eternity without ever eating a single piece of cheesecake?"

Monica looked at her husband and frowned. What was that maddening, unreadable expression on his face? "I'm going to talk to the bishop. We need to have marriage counseling."

Gordon nodded slowly. "Yes, I think you're right about that."

Monica glared at him. He was making this all look like *her* problem. He reached into the cookie jar and pulled out an Oreo, biting off part of it casually. Monica wanted to hit him. "Are you telling me *God* masturbates? That Jesus does?"

Gordon shrugged. "Well, the scriptures are silent on the issue. So who knows? But since it isn't a sin, I don't see why they wouldn't if they felt like it."

Monica's eyes narrowed. She was through with the conversation. Through with Gordon. No one who held such apostate thoughts was ever likely to fully repent. She gritted her teeth as she thought of all those wasted years. It was going to be hard to attract another man at her age. But she'd be meeting new people at work. And by definition, anyone trying to build their year's supply was dedicated to following the Prophet. She'd have to start exercising regularly to speed up her weight loss, at least a fifteen minute walk a day, even in the Utah heat. She couldn't wait to try out the treadmill.

She thought about the blasphemous accusation Gordon had just made. Heavenly Father and Jesus had dozens of wives. Maybe hundreds. Why would they ever need to do such a crude thing? What was the world coming to when a man married in the temple was defending the most selfish and debased of sexual acts? No wonder Gordon still wasn't a High Priest. Their leaders had the spirit of discernment.

"If sex is only for procreation," Gordon went on, "you've been sinning as much as I have for the past sixteen years."

Monica stood and started walking. "I'm going to my room. You're sleeping on the sofa tonight."

She stormed into the bedroom and shut the door firmly behind her, clicking the lock loudly. She sat on the bed, making the frame creak in protest, and fumed. But then she tried to breathe slowly. She had to calm down and stay married until she was in the new house, or the judge wouldn't give it to her. She wanted to call Jenny, the Relief Society president, but how could she tell anyone else about Gordon's depravity? Jenny would look at her with pity every time she saw her. Monica couldn't bear it. And she certainly couldn't talk to the bishop. How would she be able to resist asking him if Gordon was right about men?

It might be true, of course. Why else would there be one god for every two hundred goddesses? Even among Mormons, there just weren't many righteous men. Perhaps only one or two in an entire ward. Maybe in an entire stake.

But she'd find one. She'd lose weight, earn the money for her surgery, and be beautiful. Just like her new house. There had to be at least one truly good man in Provo. They'd marry in the temple in their pure white robes and slippers, their green aprons a symbol of their chastity. It would be a holy marriage this time.

Monica was going to the Celestial Kingdom.

She reached into her bedside drawer and pulled out a Ho Ho.

The Gathering 2

"Are you quite through?" asked Nellie when Quinn had finished speaking. All eyes were on Nellie. Gavin wasn't sure if she would walk over to the gun behind the ficus tree and use it on their guest herself.

"The story wasn't about you," Quinn returned with a laugh.

"Food storage. An older married couple. Right."

"But you're not fat," Gavin pointed out.

"Damn right I'm not," Nellie replied. Not technically, Gavin thought, though she did carry a few extra pounds. Of course, that was hardly a sin at her age. The fact that she had even one minor weakness at all was instead a source of comfort to him.

"So it's not us," he said. "It's just a story." He didn't need to tell her about his own masturbation, which he pretty much only did on his birthday these days. At least he didn't do it looking at pornography like some men did. He wasn't that far gone.

He stole a glance at Jon. Of course, he did think about a lot of the other priesthood holders while abusing himself. But no one was perfect. At least he'd never actually had sex with anyone besides Nellie. He made a vow to himself right at that moment he wouldn't beat off even once more before the Second Coming of Christ.

He frowned. Perhaps that wasn't the best expression to use.

For that matter, the term "holding the priesthood" had always led his mind to wander, too. And singing in Sacrament about holding onto "the iron rod." It seemed odd, Gavin thought, that Church leaders in Salt Lake, who seemed eternally committed to safeguarding the sexual purity of the other members, somehow never seemed to notice the specific phrases they used every day.

Maybe Gavin was the only man who let those phrases fill his mind with sin, he thought. He was a terrible pervert. He deserved to be killed before the Millennium started.

Nellie was still looking at Quinn, her right eyebrow arched. "I'd appreciate it if there was no more talk of food," she said. "We've got plenty, but there's no need to focus on it. We don't want to get fat while waiting for Jesus."

Quinn coughed. "Anyone else have a better story to tell?" she asked.

"You should tell us why you haven't mentioned your husband once since you arrived," Emma said. "You seem pretty cold-hearted."

Quinn stopped rocking. "If you're talking about the father of my baby," she said in a calm, deliberate manner, "I hope he's dead."

"What?" asked Jon.

Quinn looked at him carefully. "It was David, your best bud."

"He never told me anything about having a baby."

"He probably never told you he raped me, either, did he?"

There was dead silence in the room. Not even the baby was murmuring.

"He asked me on a date," Quinn continued, "I said yes, and he forced himself on me. When I told the bishop, I was disfellowshipped." She stared at Jon with narrowed eyes. "Nothing happened to David."

"I—I don't know what to say," Jon spluttered.

"Of course you don't."

Jon opened his mouth and then closed it again.

"I hope the bishop starves to death," Quinn said. "He told me I'd be excommunicated if I had an abortion." She paused. "And as for David—"

Emma jumped to her feet. "People! People! It's the Last Days! Christ is about to return! Let's all be good to each other! We need to stop talking about these awful, awful things!"

"What do *you* want to talk about?" asked Quinn with a slight sneer. Then, seeming to remember what had just happened to Emma, she closed her eyes, regrouped, and put on a more supportive face. Gavin had learned to keep a blank face years ago. It was the only safe way to get through life.

"I'll take care of you, Quinn," Jon said softly.

"Like you did when you made me come out from behind the rose bush first?"

Jon looked at the floor.

"Stop it, stop it, stop it!" said Emma. "Someone else tell a story. Anything."

No one said a word. Finally, after several long moments, Gavin turned to Emma and nodded. "Perhaps you'd better tell us something, dear," he said.

She nodded back. "Okay, I will." She furrowed her brows and looked about the room, as if hoping some object would spark her imagination. Her eyes rested for a moment on a doily Nellie had crocheted years before. Then her expression changed and she leaned back. "Here's my story," she said.

A Beehive in the House

Marta could hardly wait for the class to begin. She was finally a Beehive instructor, a calling she'd wanted for years. She'd been afraid that when she announced her first pregnancy two months earlier at the age of twenty-eight, the bishop would assign her to the Nursery, but he really was inspired. Marta was teaching the Beehives. She glanced down at the cloth Kroger shopping bag beside her classroom table, with her blue steel lockbox inside.

"Good morning, Sister Crowley," Elizabeth said as she walked into the room. The thirteen-year-old sat right in the middle of the front row. The girl was tall for her age and well-developed, but she was as sweet and gentle as a lamb. Marta saw her every week in Sacrament meeting. The girl brought real scriptures with her, not an iPhone.

"Good to see you, Elizabeth."

Anya and Nidelfa came through the door next and sat in the row behind Elizabeth and off to the side. They didn't say anything to either Elizabeth or Marta. Marta smiled at them benevolently.

Marta looked at the clock on the wall. It was already one minute past starting time. She was just trying to think of some kind of small talk she could initiate when Cathy and Barbara rushed in, sitting to the left of Elizabeth. Marta stood and shut the door. Classes were small out in the mission field. She'd been lucky to meet Kyle at BYU. She knew that. But she wished he'd asked her opinion before taking a job offer in Houston.

Or before buying their house.

But she wasn't blind. She saw the way single women in the ward looked at Kyle. She saw other women in the grocery store, and at the post office, or at the bank, stuck with their mediocre, uninspired husbands. She knew how lucky she was to have a priesthood holder to call her own.

"Good morning, girls," Marta began. "As you know, I'm your new teacher, and I'm going to start our time together by presenting my absolute favorite lesson I ever had when I was your age."

"Don't think you'll be here very long, do you?" asked Anya. Nidelfa snickered. She was Filipino.

"You're not going to make us bake cupcakes, are you?" asked Barbara. She had amazingly blond hair that looked natural. Marta was jealous. Kyle insisted on Marta bleaching her own hair.

Of course, it wasn't as if he didn't do things for her in return. Just last week, he'd edged the lawn without being prodded.

"What's the lesson about, Sister Crowley?" Elizabeth asked with a smile.

"It's about time travel," Marta replied, waiting to see everyone's reaction. Anya rolled her eyes. Cathy and Barbara looked at each other in confusion. Elizabeth looked up at Marta sweetly.

"We're not going to wear old-fashioned clothes, are we?" asked Anya.

Marta thought she heard Nidelfa say something, the word "you" at the end of it. Anya and Nidelfa snickered.

Marta grabbed the shopping bag by its handles and set it on the table with a clunk. Even the annoying girls were intrigued, Marta could tell. She reached in and slowly pulled out the lockbox, setting it down so the girls could see the heavy lock on the front.

"What is it?" asked Barbara.

"It's a time capsule," Marta replied. She took a key out of her purse and opened the lid. The girls craned their necks to look inside. Anya even stood up to see.

"What's the letter say?" asked Anya.

Marta picked up the single envelope gingerly from inside the box and set it down on the table. "It's a letter my Beehive instructor made me write many years ago."

"Many," Anya whispered to Nidelfa. They covered their mouths.

"I told myself I wouldn't read it until the day I was a Beehive teacher myself. I've been tempted many times but I waited. It's important to always keep your commitments. I waited the same way you can wait for your first kiss. The way you can wait to fully express your love until you're married to a righteous man in the temple."

Elizabeth smiled sweetly at Marta and nodded.

"What we're all going to do today," Marta continued, "is write a letter to our future selves. You'll write what you want in a husband, and what you want out of marriage."

Anya rolled her eyes.

Kyle had told Marta not to teach the lesson. "Mormon girls don't want real men," he said. "They want princes. Teach them something useful like how to make mashed potatoes without lumps. Don't fill their heads with an ideal they'll never attain."

Marta never had lumps in her potatoes. She squeezed her own orange juice, too.

One could only get to the Celestial Kingdom if their temple marriage was a success. It was a team effort.

"I'm going to do something different than my own Beehive teacher did," Marta continued. "I'm going to collect all your letters and place them in this lockbox along with mine. And I'll keep them until you're all married. I'll give them back to you on your first wedding anniversary, and you'll be shocked—shocked—to see just how accurate your predictions were."

"How are you going to get it to me?" asked Nidelfa. "What if I'm away at college?"

"What if I move to Los Angeles to be a singer?" asked Barbara.

"What if I'm inactive in the Church?" asked Cathy.

"The Church always knows where you are," Marta said with a smile. Anya and Nidelfa exchanged glances.

"I'm only twelve," said Cathy. "How am I supposed to know what I want? I can't even date for four more years yet."

Marta stroked the blue steel gently, as if petting a cat. The action made the girls keep their focus on her. "You wouldn't start high school without having gone to elementary and middle school first," she said. "You wouldn't go to college without finishing high school. You certainly don't start a marriage without having thought about it ahead of time. It's the most important decision you'll ever make in your entire lives. So it's never too early to begin planning."

Marta remembered Kyle telling her in front of the Harold B. Lee Library that he'd received a personal revelation she should marry him. She'd always dreamed of marrying someone who might one day be a General Authority. It was important to plan one's life this specifically, so one would be ready when the right opportunity arose. Imagine if she'd only been thinking about marrying a good-looking man. Or someone who always brought her flowers. Where would she be right now?

"I want crab cakes at my reception," said Anya. Everyone giggled except Elizabeth, who sat calmly looking at Marta, a contented smile on her face.

"These goals will stay with you forever," Marta promised. "They are a part of you. And what's so wonderful about this project is that it not only forces you to focus on healthy objectives, but it also demonstrates to you how good you really are deep inside already." She looked at Anya. "Even when you pretend not to be."

"It sounds like an absolutely lovely lesson, Sister Crowley." Elizabeth moved the scriptures on her desk off to the corner to make room for writing.

Marta took out a thin box of special stationery she'd bought for the occasion and handed each girl two sheets of paper with purple violets along the top. Then she handed everyone ink pens. The options were blue, green, pink, and purple. She knew how to be a fun teacher. That's why the bishop had called her.

"Ah, lavender," said Elizabeth, holding a sheet of the paper to her nose.

"Start writing," said Marta. "Write what you want most in the world. No one else is ever going to see these letters besides you." She sat down behind the table and caressed the blue steel box again. "I can tell you, I've often wished I could write a letter now and send it back in time to my twelve-year-old self. But that kind of time travel isn't possible. What you *can* do, though, is tell your twenty-one-year-old self something important."

Anya and Nidelfa looked at each other, Cathy and Barbara looked at each other, and Elizabeth looked serenely at Marta. Marta nodded, and they all turned to their paper.

Now it was Marta's turn to do something. She carefully examined the envelope from the lockbox. She'd brought a special letter opener for the occasion, with a series of small lilies on the handle. She quietly ripped through the fold of the envelope. Anya looked up in annoyance at the distraction. Marta carefully pulled out the letter and unfolded it.

"I want a marriage that will last through the eternities," she read. She stopped, struck by the maturity she'd demonstrated. Even as a child she knew how to set priorities. She continued. "I want a man with an unwavering testimony of the gospel." It was uncanny. She'd gotten exactly what she wanted, without ever having reread the letter in the eight years that passed before she met her husband.

She would have to prepare some watermelon for Kyle's dessert later, to show her appreciation. He would only eat the fruit if she cut it into bite-size pieces, removing even the tiny white seeds in "seedless" watermelons.

Marta wondered why Kyle spoke so disparagingly of Mormon girls wanting princes. Kyle *was* a prince, and she was lucky to have him. When he told her to polish his dress shoes every Saturday, she was happy to do it. He always made sure to give *her* a special gift Saturday night.

She touched her right nipple absentmindedly, where Kyle had bit down a little too hard the night before.

After about fifteen minutes, the girls seemed to be through with their assignment and were talking and giggling to each other, probably about the latest decadent pop star in trouble with the law again. Marta didn't understand why people couldn't obey the simplest of laws.

She tapped the steel box and stood up. "Okay, class. I've written your names on these envelopes, and now I'd like you each to put your letter in your envelope and seal it in front of everyone. As I said before, the letters will remain sealed until your first wedding anniversary. I'll keep them safe in this lockbox until then." She collected the sealed envelopes, put them in the lockbox next to her own letter which she'd returned, and turned the key in the lock. The class spent the remaining few minutes of the period discussing the history of the Relief Society.

It was amazing how little Mormon girls knew these days.

Marta drove back home and carried the heavy shopping bag into the house. "Hi, honey," she said. "I'm home."

"I'm watching the game," Kyle replied, not even looking up.

Marta stood and debated what to say next. She could turn this into a romantic moment. They might make love two days in a row. She liked those little proofs their marriage was a success. "My lesson went well," she said, absentmindedly rubbing her behind, where Kyle had forced himself in a little too roughly the night before.

"I'm watching the game," Kyle repeated.

Marta looked at him, a bag of Funyons in his lap, a can of Red Bull on the coffee table in front of him. She headed back for her tiny office at the rear of the house. She pulled out the lockbox and set it on her desk. Marta wanted to read her letter once more, but somehow she felt she should wait several more years before looking at it again. Still, she needed to do *something* to complete the special activity in her mind.

She unlocked the box and looked at the other letters, lifting them one by one and turning them casually in her hand. Actually, she thought now, she had lots of unused envelopes left over. She could write the girls' names on five more, open these envelopes, and read the letters. Then she could reseal the letters in the new envelopes. The girls would never know. It would be a bit sneaky, but as their moral guide, she needed to know that the girls were on the straight and narrow, and perhaps there was no other way than to read what they'd written.

Marta picked up her letter opener again and decided to read Anya's letter first. She was clearly the girl who needed the most monitoring. Marta pulled out the letter and read.

"I want a man with a big dick, at least eight inches long," Marta read, her mouth opening in horror. "So I'll demand to see it before we get married. In fact, I want to know sex is going to be good, so we'll have sex even before we're engaged." Marta was mortified. She was going to have to talk to Anya's parents. Or the bishop.

But how could she do that without revealing she'd read the letter? Marta stared at the paper in her hand. There was just no getting out of it, she decided. She'd have to say the Spirit urged her to read what Anya had written.

The letter went on and on, describing sexual features and acts in detail. Marta couldn't put the letter down, fidgeting in her chair. Then at the end, it said, "April Fool, Sister Crowley. I knew you'd read this!"

Marta's face flushed, and she put the letter down. What a horrid child. Such a lying, manipulative…

She slipped the letter into a new envelope, wrote Anya's name on the front, and sealed it shut. Perhaps she shouldn't read any of the others. She closed the lid and turned the key in the lock, setting the box on the floor beside her desk. She logged onto the computer and read her email. Then she checked the ward website. Maybe she should send a care package to that nice young elder serving in Uruguay.

She started thinking about what she might include. Kyle would be upset at the waste of money, but it was important to do good deeds. One had to be loving to reach the Celestial Kingdom. Kyle said so every Monday night during Family Home Evening when he made her suck him off.

A few minutes later, Marta looked down at the lockbox again. She really needed something to lift her spirits. It couldn't hurt to read Elizabeth's letter, could it? She nudged the box with her toes, turned away and ignored it, and then nudged it with her toes again. After a few moments, she lifted the lockbox back onto the desk. She casually unlocked it and picked up Elizabeth's letter. Marta turned it over and over in her fingers, pulling it closer to her, starting to put it back, and then pulling it closer to her again.

She picked up her letter opener and slit the envelope. Lilies were so lovely. Pulling out the letter, Marta took a deep breath and began reading.

"I want a man who will help me reach the Celestial Kingdom," it began, and Marta relaxed with a smile. "I want a man who has an unbreakable testimony of the gospel, as I have." Marta sighed and continued. She felt the way she felt when she drank a cold Sprite on a hot Texas day.

"I want a sister wife like Marta Crowley," the letter went on, and Marta stopped breathing. "I want to marry a man like Kyle Crowley, even if I'm a second wife. Or a third, or a fourth. I will wait for Brother Crowley as long as it takes, just as he said he'll wait for me. With gay marriage legal now, he told me, it's only a matter of time before polygamy is legal again. God works in mysterious ways."

Marta wondered if Elizabeth were playing a prank, too, like Anya had done. She heard a buzzing near the window and saw that a bee had become trapped in the house. She hated watching bees die slowly, unable to escape. She watched for several minutes as the bee bumped up repeatedly against the glass, not understanding why this clear substance wasn't air.

Marta sealed the letter back in a fresh envelope, put all the letters back in the lockbox, and turned the key. Then she stood up and calmly walked back to the living room. Kyle ate the last Funyon out of the bag and tossed the bag onto the coffee table, taking another swig of his Red Bull. His eyes never left the television screen.

Marta moved softly in the kitchen so as not to disturb her husband and then walked quietly up behind him. She waited until he shouted in victory when his team scored a point. No one passing by outside would have heard anything other than that victory yell when she plunged the knife into his back. She'd leave the back door ajar for the police to discover after letting them in through the front later, when she called in an hour or two.

She turned off the TV before walking to the bedroom. She lay on the bed, picked up her Deseret romance from the bedside table, and began reading where she'd left off the night before.

The Gathering 3

"Ha!" shouted Quinn, then looked nervously to make sure she hadn't awakened the baby. "Way to go, Emma!" she said more softly.

"You sure it was the bishop who killed Eric?" Jon asked nervously.

Emma smiled. "It's just a story."

"Sure it is," said Nellie. She put her embroidery down and rubbed her eyes. In the dim candlelight, it was apparently too difficult to continue.

Emma shrugged. "I'll admit, Eric was a big baby. Made such a fuss even when he had a minor cold. Believe me, I'll manage the Apocalypse a lot better without him."

"True love if ever I heard it," Nellie said.

Emma shrugged again. "It's not like he won't be waiting for me on the Other Side. I'm just saying some things are easier without husbands tagging along." She looked at Gavin.

Gavin felt uncomfortable and decided to lighten the mood. "You've always said, Nellie, you prefer grocery shopping without me." Nellie glared at him as if he'd just betrayed her. He shut up.

"I'm having a fun time," Quinn said with a smile. "Storytelling was a good idea, Jon."

"It's kind of like the pioneers singing 'Put your shoulder to the wheel' as they crossed the plains." He looked at Emma and Nellie and then Gavin, but he wasn't smiling.

"Anyone want something to drink?" asked Nellie, standing up. "You can have tap water or tap water," she said. "We're saving the bottled and canned drinks until the water cuts off."

"What if the tap water has bacteria?" asked Quinn.

"Then we'll die," Nellie replied. "Drinks, anyone?"

Everyone nodded their assent, and Nellie soon returned with a tray of clear plastic glasses in various colors of the rainbow, all filled with tepid water. Nellie took the yellow glass, her favorite color. It looked like she was drinking urine. Gavin took a sip from his glass. It probably looked like he was drinking grape juice. He sure hoped everyone didn't end up with diarrhea. Even with running water, that would make for some unpleasant company.

Nellie sat back down, looking as if she'd like nothing more than to continue her embroidery. But she leaned back and said, "How about we hear a *nice* story this time?" The look she gave made Gavin hope no one turned down her offer. No one did, and she began speaking.

Car Keys in the Hands of an Angry God

It was time to head to Relief Society. Teaching was a burden, but it naturally fell on the gifted. Yet Ava wasn't going to be able to teach anyone if she couldn't get to the chapel. She sighed heavily and fished about in her purse again. She set her lips and looked on the counter. She ran back to the bedroom and searched the top of her dresser. Where were those frickin' car keys?

Ava gritted her teeth and checked the bathroom. Nothing. She was not the type to misplace things. All the cans in her food storage were facing forward, in alphabetical order. Beets (halved), beets (pickled), beets (sliced), black-eyed peas, and so forth. She was called the Divining Rod of the neighborhood because she always knew where to tell people to look for a lost pet. She could even find a missing Viagra tablet, when Greg thought the bottle was empty.

Gosh darn it. Ava was supposed to teach the Compassionate Service lesson today. She had everything planned, about how a mother replaced her daughter's birth control pills with baby aspirin to teach her how wrong it was to have premarital sex. The girl had still been living at home, after all, and still obligated to live by her parents' rules. Ava hadn't quite understood how the mother managed to fake the pills, since as she understood it, the real ones came in a specific packet, but she'd read the story in a reputable religious magazine and felt it worth sharing. If you could call a fundamentalist Christian magazine reputable. It wasn't as if they had the one true church or anything.

Dagnabbit. Where were those car keys?

After searching every spot she could think of, Ava knew there was no other choice. She knelt down beside her purse and bowed her head. She hated asking Heavenly Father for help until after she'd done all she could on her own. But He'd given her the task of teaching this lesson, and she remembered Nephi's promise in chapter three, verse seven. If Heavenly Father wanted her to do His bidding, He had to do His part now.

So she prayed. And in a flash, she *knew* where those car keys were. Ava stood up and walked directly to her closet. She opened the door, and there they were on the floor. She remembered now dropping her purse while she was trying to decide which dress to wear with the new bag.

"Found my keys!" Ava shouted on her way to the kitchen.

Greg was sitting at the table, where he'd been ignoring her frantic running about. "Without the help of an angel?" he said, taking a bite out of a cold chicken leg.

"Oh, ye of little faith," she returned with a smile. She went over to give him a kiss anyway. She was on her way to teach others about compassion, after all.

"Don't know why Heavenly Father didn't help me sink that putt," Greg replied. "If I'd impressed the boss, I might have gotten that raise you keep insisting on." He licked a finger.

Ava was not going to be dragged back into a discussion about God again. Greg had been missing more and more church lately, avoiding the scriptures, and even watching TV on Sunday. Once he actually came home from a morning jog with coffee on his breath. If he didn't snap out of this mood soon, she was going to insist on marriage counseling.

"You forget that Heavenly Father helped you get that job in the first place," said Ava. "After the bishop recommended you."

"To his friend who pays slave wages."

"Slaves don't make wages."

Greg took another bite of his chicken. "Enjoy your meeting."

Now Ava was irritated. He was trying to get rid of her. As if *she* were the problem. It was just like a man. She stole a quick glance at her watch. She was already late, but if she sped through the two school zones on her way to church and didn't get caught, it wouldn't be too bad. It wasn't as if there were any kids there right now. She felt inspired to say something else.

"I'm going to give you a challenge," she said.

"An ice bucket challenge?" he replied. "I can think of one I'd like to give you, too."

Ava shook her head, not rising to the bait. "The Book of Moroni challenge," she said. "Pray while I'm away, with all your heart, and ask Heavenly Father what I should cook you for dinner."

"Huh?"

"It'll show you that Heavenly Father truly cares about *you*." She smiled. "Even the fall of a sparrow."

Greg frowned but nodded. And it was a win/win situation. Greg always wanted lasagna when he could get it. Since it was so much trouble, Ava only prepared it on special occasions. But she always had the ingredients on hand for when she needed to pull a rabbit out of a hat. She'd show him that Heavenly Father answered prayers. Just like He'd shown her where to find her car keys. She was strong. She'd help him rebuild his testimony.

Flippin' heck. Now she *was* going to be late. Ava kissed Greg once more, grabbed her teaching manual and Christian magazine, and hurried out the door. She climbed into the car and backed up without warming the engine.

She had to go faster than the speed limit on these residential streets to make up time. 20 miles an hour was ridiculous in any event. She rolled past a stop sign and ran a red light after looking both ways while merging onto the main road, and before long, she'd made up a few minutes of the commute. Olivia Newton-John was singing, "Let Me Be There." Ava only listened to Olivia's old music. Before the woman fell into sin with those decadent lyrics of the '80's. She sang along with the CD. And then it happened.

Right in front of her was Sally Briggs, doing her make-up in the mirror, late for church as usual. To Ava's horror, the woman veered right into the oncoming lane and hit a pick-up truck head on. The sound of ripping metal and shattering glass was both terrifying and sickening. Ava stopped her car and jumped out to see what she could do.

She was the Compassionate Service leader.

Sally's arm looked broken, and even the air bag hadn't prevented several serious lacerations. "Ava," the woman muttered helplessly, looking up at Ava in a daze. "Help me."

If Ava hadn't misplaced her car keys, she wouldn't have been late. She might have been exactly where Sister Briggs was now. Heavenly Father had *saved* her. She felt a tingle down her spine as the Spirit testified to her.

"Sally, I'll call your husband."

Sally moaned. "Call a goddamn ambulance."

Ava frowned. It was so sad when others let trials make them lose their principles. She ran back to her car and dialed Brother Briggs and then the bishop and Relief Society president. There were other people around to call 9-1-1. After only a few moments, she could hear sirens approaching. She went back to comfort Sally.

"I don't have the priesthood," Ava said softly, "but I can still bless you with this message: Heavenly Father has given you this experience to help you grow stronger. It's for your own good." She paused. "If you pass this test, Heavenly Father might even see that you finally get pregnant again."

Sally then said a very bad word. Ava shook her head in amazement. It was not only sad but also mystifying to see people crumble under the slightest strain. Here Ava was faced with losing her husband of thirty years to a temple divorce if he didn't repent, and she was still strong. Why did others have to be so weak?

A moment later, an ambulance pulled up, and two uniformed men jumped out. The driver of the pick-up truck didn't seem badly injured, so the men directed their attention to Sally. Ava looked at her watch. "I've got to go teach Relief Society," she said as the first paramedic leaned over Sally. "I'll stop by the hospital later to give you a recap."

A police car pulled up right at that moment, and one of the officers tried to get Ava to tell him what had happened, but she explained she had an emergency of her own and jumped into her car. She could always give a statement later. It wasn't as if she had been involved in the accident in any way and was obligated to stay.

She was hopelessly late at this point and probably shouldn't have wasted so much time as it was, but you had to be a good person, didn't you? Still, it wasn't fair to penalize the other sisters by depriving them of her lesson just because Sally was careless.

Ava eased around the accident scene carefully and then sped up. Two more stoplights, a four-way stop, and one more long residential street, and she was almost at the chapel. Then, to her horror, a black toy poodle walked right out in front of her. She felt the soft impact and pulled over immediately.

Ava stood looking at the dead animal in the street and wiped away a tear. So terribly, terribly tragic. And Heavenly Father cared even about the fall of a sparrow, she remembered telling Greg. No one else was outside just now on this residential block, so no one had seen what had happened.

Then Ava remembered that animals went to the Celestial Kingdom if they fulfilled the measure of their creation. So there was no real need to spend any more time on the incident. She tried to compose herself, let out a deep breath, and climbed back in her car. She stepped on the gas and continued quickly on her way. The other sisters would be waiting for her lesson.

And after everything that had happened, Ava was in the mood to teach it well. It never failed to amaze her, she thought, pulling into the church parking lot. Heavenly Father always directed her in each of her callings. It was downright astonishing to have so much evidence every day that the gospel was true.

Ava grabbed her materials, climbed out of her car, and hurried to the building with a smile.

The Gathering 4

There was silence when Nellie stopped speaking. She picked up her yellow plastic cup and took another sip of her water. Gavin looked about at the others in the living room. They had clearly heard something different than Nellie believed she had said. It would be so much easier to be a good Mormon, he thought, if good Mormons weren't so clueless.

Was he clueless?

He looked over at Jon and wondered what it would have been like to kiss another man even one single time in his entire life.

The Millennium had better damn well be worth all this, he thought.

"Any granola bars?" asked Emma. "Or whatever else you guys have in food storage?"

"Yes, perhaps we'd better eat before it gets too late," Nellie agreed. "I'll open a few cans of green beans and Vienna sausage and heat it all on the stove."

Jon looked a little sickened by the announcement. Gavin wondered just how far off the Second Coming would be. They'd always been told to have enough to last a year on hand, and the ultra-righteous like Nellie had insisted on enough for two years. But Gavin sincerely hoped all the extra was just to ensure the faithful had plenty to feed their faithless neighbors. He certainly didn't want to believe they might really have to live like this for an entire year or more.

"Green beans and Vienna sausage?" asked Quinn. "You did say you're the Relief Society president?"

"Feel free to go outside and graze," Nellie returned.

"You're right, Sister Askew," Quinn replied in a softer voice. "I'm being a bitch. I apologize." Nellie lit another candle and walked off to the kitchen with a triumphant smile. Harper was fussing a little, so Quinn moved over and changed her diaper. She'd brought a pile of spares from the back to the living room earlier, along with a can of wipes. When she finished changing the baby, she looked about in confusion.

"We'll put it out in the garbage behind the house," Gavin said. "Come on."

They passed Nellie in the kitchen, who didn't give them so much as a glance, and then returned to the living room. There was finally some talk about the war, or the terrorist attack, or whatever had happened, but no one wanted to dwell on the subject very long. "I do wish I'd bought a handcart on one of the Prepper sites," Emma said, "so I could get back to Jackson County."

"Kansas City was hit, too, you know," Jon said softly.

"Yes, but Jackson County…"

Jon shook his head. Everyone looked at each other hopelessly.

"I wonder how my parents are," Quin mused, rocking the baby back to sleep.

"Mine died of the plague," Emma said.

No one spoke for the next several minutes. Then they heard Nellie call out from the kitchen. "Emma, come help me serve." Watching her head down the dark hallway, Gavin wondered why he'd never thought to install gas lighting for situations like this.

He thought about Ingrid Bergman.

They ate mostly in silence, the only sound the clinking of forks against plates. When they were finished, Nellie said, "You wash the dishes, Quinn. We'll use the real plates until the water goes out. Then we have paper plates for the duration." She looked at Gavin as if evaluating the task ahead of her.

"And we'll endure to the end," he said, forcing a smile. "We're all going to make it to the Celestial Kingdom. It's not the end of the world."

Quinn laughed and shook her head before handing the baby to Jon and marching to the kitchen. When she was finished, Jon eagerly gave Harper back to her mother, and everyone sat staring at Quinn rocking in her chair. Quinn looked back at everyone, perturbed at the attention.

"I guess it's time for another story," said Gavin, trying to sound cheery. "I suppose it's my turn now."

"Be my guest," said Nellie. "If you think you can top mine."

"It's not a contest," said Emma. "We're just trying to get through the day."

Gavin realized he hadn't heard any gunshots or screams in a while. He thought about all the long years he'd spent with Nellie, and the countless eons they would spend together in the eternities. He looked at Jon, who had the cutest ears. Gavin flexed his fingers and nodded to no one in particular. And then he began to tell his story.

Living a Cher Song

I suppose it should have been obvious to anyone, but my wife never seemed to suspect. My bishops over the years never suspected. Nor my kids or coworkers. As far as I knew, no one at all had suspected until this morning when I went to wait for my newspaper. I still had the print version of the *Deseret News* delivered right to my doorstep.

It was 5:00 a.m. and I was already up on a Saturday morning. Debbie never understood why I didn't want to sleep late on the weekends when I was blissfully liberated from my job in downtown Salt Lake. I'd explained that I didn't want to waste even one precious second of my free time not being completely conscious of that second.

"Hey there," the paperboy said as he tossed the newspaper out of his van. The "paperboy" looked to be in his mid-thirties, with a scraggly beard and a torn T-shirt. I'd seen him drive by on other mornings, too. I nodded politely in response. The van stopped, and the driver waved for me to approach. When I did, he leaned out his window. "No one's up yet. How about I pull over and we get in the back of the van for a few minutes?" He pointed behind him with his thumb and grinned.

I must have looked confused because he laughed and said, "Come on. I don't usually give it up for old guys, but you look like you could use a good fuck."

My mouth fell open.

"You'd rather suck me off?" The man shrugged. "That'll do, too, though I was really in the mood for fucking. I'll pull right over."

There was some room along the curb in front of the neighbor's house, and the van pulled off to the side of the street. The driver stepped out and waved me over. He opened the back door of the van and motioned me inside. I climbed in and he followed, shutting the door behind us.

Six minutes later, it was all over. I'd had sex with another man for the first time in my life, at the age of fifty-five. With a complete stranger I expected I wouldn't even like if I knew him very well. He'd had some hand lotion ready for situations like this and slid right inside me. I felt complete for the first time. I hadn't wanted it to end.

360 seconds of acute awareness later, it was.

I stepped out of the van and the driver continued on his morning route without so much as a wave goodbye. And suddenly, I felt like crying. Perhaps I hadn't wasted any of my valuable Saturday morning, but I now began to wonder if I'd instead wasted my entire worthless life.

Back inside, I started frying some bacon. Debbie liked bacon on the weekends. Real bacon, not that turkey stuff. It showed on both of our midlines. But it wasn't as if we were trying to look good for each other. We probably only had sex once a month.

I put five strips of cooked bacon on a saucer and set it on the table where Debbie always sat. She wouldn't be up for another half hour. But I was already dressed and felt too anxious to stay in the house. I stepped into the car parked in the driveway and pulled out, heading downtown. Downtown on a Saturday. Temple Square was going to be too overwhelming after what had just happened, but I needed something Mormon in my life to remind me of my vows. I meandered down several streets, through the neighborhoods, back and forth and around, and finally found myself parking near the Seagull Monument.

I walked up to the statue and thought about the miracle of Heavenly Father's intervention over the years in the lives of the saints. A seagull perched on the top of the seagull. Unusual since we were so far from the lake. Maybe it was a sign.

"Heavenly Father," I prayed in a soft whisper, though there was no one else around. The words of an old Eddie Money song came flooding into my head and out of my mouth. "I want to go back." As I said it, I felt an invisible hand squeezing my heart inside my chest. "My Lord my God, what am I going to do?"

It was almost 6:30 now and the city was beginning to wake up. A car drove by with its windows down, and I could hear yet another '80's song drifting into the air. Cher was singing, "If I could turn back time."

It couldn't be a coincidence.

I vaguely remembered a children's story I'd read decades ago, about a girl and a boy on a subway in New York, the girl irritated at the great mass of people. She'd heard that if you made a wish at a certain place in the first car of the subway, your wish would be granted. She wished to go someplace in the city that wasn't so crowded. And poof, she and her brother were whisked back to New Amsterdam before the city turned into the sprawling metropolis it eventually became.

I looked up at the golden seagull on the column before me. "I want to go back to Italy and marry my mission president," I whispered.

Nothing happened.

I stepped a few inches to my right and repeated the wish. Then I moved over a little more and repeated it again. I continued all the way around the monument, wishing, wishing. Finally, I was back where I'd started. "I want to go back…" I began, and suddenly I was flying through a dark tunnel with a light at the far end of it.

My Lord my God!

Did I have a heart attack, I wondered, even without my own share of bacon this morning? Was I dying and going to the Other Side? This was hardly what I was hoping for, but maybe death was better than going back to the house.

Now the light at the end of the tunnel was dimming. I could no longer see anything at all. Everything turned black.

***

"You okay, Anziano Russell?"

I felt groggy. Who was talking?

"Stai bene?" the voice repeated.

"Huh?"

"Let me help you up, Anziano."

I felt arms lifting me to my feet. It was dark outside, nighttime. I looked about in bewilderment. There was a cheese shop across the street. And next to it a bread shop. I swung around and stared at the man who had helped me. It was Elder Alsop.

I was back in Rome Four.

I looked about. There was my old apartment on Via Franco Sacchetti. There on the corner was the little bar where we always stopped to get milk and cookies.

I grabbed Elder Alsop's arm. I could feel him. This was real.

"That was quite a fall you took, Elder," my companion said. "Can you make it back to the apartment?"

"Sí," I said. "Sto bene. Posso camminare. Andiamo." I remembered my Italian as if I'd just left my mission yesterday.

We walked slowly back to our building, Elder Alsop supporting my left arm, though I really didn't need any help. I just liked the touch, even through suit jackets. I remembered now that Elder Alsop had been my favorite companion of the eleven I'd had during my time in Italy.

We hadn't spoken in almost thirty-five years.

Back in the apartment, we greeted the other four elders who'd already returned home for the evening and went straight to our room, tossing our scriptures and flip charts onto our desks. I changed into my jeans and red plaid shirt, and Elder Alsop simply stripped down to his garments.

I'd forgotten we used to wear one-piece garments. I looked at my companion in admiration. How many other guys found men wearing old-fashioned Mormon underwear sexy? I must really be a pervert.

I nodded. That was why I was here. My mission—to tell the only man I'd ever loved we were meant to be together. "Elder Alsop," I said, "I need to go to the mission home tomorrow morning."

"What?" He shook his head. "The sisters are coming over at 10:00 so we can all finish working on the new mostra." He was talking about the decorated wooden streetboard we used in order to attract passersby on the sidewalk, a technique which rarely worked but which allowed us to stand by idly talking to each other while pretending to proselytize. We were just finishing putting together a new and improved mostra, like the latest version of Tide detergent. I tried to think back on what period we'd done that.

I remembered. It was clear I'd gone back in time to late March the last year of my mission. Elder Alsop and I were just about to meet the Ciambella family sometime in the next few days. We'd end up baptizing the entire family of five.

"I need to talk to President Fowler," I said.

"What's wrong?"

"Nothing. I just need to speak to him." I remembered how in every mission interview, the president had tousled my hair, the intimate feel of his hand on my head always giving me an erection, which I tried to hide as we then talked about missionary work.

Elder Alsop came over to my bed and sat down. I looked at him and frowned but eventually sat down as well. "You don't make an appointment with the president for 'nothing,'" Elder Alsop said. "Is it me? Am I a problem to you?"

"Of course not, Anziano. We're about to baptize a family of five."

Elder Alsop raised an eyebrow.

"I mean, no, you're good. We're good."

Elder Alsop smiled hesitantly. "I know I've only been out eight months," he said, "but you're the best companion I've had so far. I don't want an emergency transfer."

I looked in his face. He was so very, very young. I remembered he'd always liked books. Hadn't he read contraband back in the day? I seemed to remember him clandestinely buying a copy of *Guerre Stellari* and a few other non-Church books.

"Did you ever finish *Star Wars* in Italian?" I asked.

"Is that what's bothering you?" he said. "I'm sorry. But it's helping me with the language. I'm reading *The Decameron* now." I vaguely remembered seeing him with a thick book in the mornings when he was supposed to be studying the missionary lessons.

"We all do what we have to to get through the day," I said. And I couldn't get through another day without President Fowler. I'd wasted so many already.

"For me to finish getting through this day," Elder Alsop said, "I need some Nutella with bread and milk." He stood up and motioned toward the bedroom door. "I'll treat if you've run out."

"Thanks, Anziano."

We had our snack, listening to the other elders tell us of their day's adventures while they snacked as well. Then Elder Alsop and I went back to our room and climbed into our separate cots. I was afraid to go to sleep, worried I'd wake up back an old man in Salt Lake. But eventually I did close my eyes, and I dreamed of kissing President Fowler.

I called the mission home in the morning, and despite some nasty looks from the zone leaders as they set up the mostra to finish their work, Elder Alsop and I left the apartment at 9:30 and caught the 106 to Piazza Sempione. From there, we had to walk the rest of the way to Via Cimone.

One of the assistants to the president opened the door. He would become a newscaster for Fox later, an impressive guy even all those years ago. Elder Alsop and I entered the house, and President Fowler came walking down the stairs. "Always happy to see you, Elder Russell," he said. "Though I must say I'm surprised. You never have problems. Hope your visit doesn't portend the end of the world." He chuckled a little nervously.

Soon we were in his office alone, and I knew this was the moment Heavenly Father had gifted to me. There would have been no reason to grant my wish halfway. If he'd sent me back in time, it was so I could finally live the life I'd wanted ever since the first day I'd met President Fowler.

"Things okay with your companion?" the president asked, tousling my hair before sitting down.

"Yes."

"The zone leaders treating you okay?"

"They're fine," I said.

"Missing the States?"

I held up both hands in front of me as if I were stopping a truck. "President," I said, "I'm fifty-five years old. Almost your age. Heavenly Father sent me back in time so we could run off together and get married."

Dead silence filled the room. I grasped my chair to remind myself I could feel it, that this was in fact all really happening. President Fowler stared at me, looked down at his desk, stared at me some more, and looked down at his desk again. I realized that he was from an earlier generation, when it was much harder to come to terms with his sexual orientation, and that it had taken me decades even as a younger man. Perhaps I should bear my testimony of what had happened.

"Elder Russell," President Fowler said slowly, "I won't send you home to be excommunicated. Your companion phoned shortly after you did and explained that you'd hit your head last night." He took a deep breath. "You go back to your apartment and rest for the next couple of days. We'll speak again after church on Sunday, and you'll tell me then that everything is back to normal."

"President…"

"You'll tell me then that everything is back to normal."

"Yes, President."

We both stood and walked toward the office door. President Fowler started to offer his hand, but then his lip curled in disgust and he withdrew it. I stumbled out into the hallway and joined my companion. We walked out of the house without another word, heading back to the open market at the piazza, where we could catch another bus.

I would have understood if the president had been afraid. I had expected that. But he wasn't afraid. He was repulsed.

"You okay, Anziano?"

I shook my head, and we kept walking. If going back in time was not enough to fix my life, I didn't understand what it was going to take. A huge truck rumbled by, and Elder Alsop pulled me further from the curb. I remembered another time, right about this same period, when I'd almost walked in front of a bus, the same day, I thought, that we'd ended up meeting the Ciambella family. I'd always taken the near tragedy as a sign that Satan was trying to stop the work. But big buses were good, I thought. Maybe I was sent back so I could die on my mission, my only hope of salvation.

We'd almost reached the piazza when Elder Alsop tripped on a piece of broken cement and fell. I heard a disturbingly hollow clunk as his head struck the pavement. My companion lay motionless on the sidewalk for a long moment, and I wondered if I'd killed him. He'd never fallen the first time around. My rewriting history was letting new events take place.

I kneeled down beside him and patted his face. "You okay, Anziano?" I asked.

His eyes fluttered open, and he tried to focus. His brows furrowed, and he frowned. Then he sat up with a jerk. "Oh, my god!" he said.

I was a little taken aback at the language but helped my companion back to his feet. "Elder Russell!" he said. "It's you! It's been so long!"

I looked at him a little queerly.

"I'm an Italian professor at Yale right now, but God sent me back to be with you."

He was talking as crazy as I'd been.

Elder Alsop laughed. "I was watching an old episode of *Star Trek*," he said. "The one where the planet is dying, and the inhabitants don't have the technology or capability to evacuate every person on the planet, so they send themselves back in time to various parts of the planet's history to live out their lives in those other times." He shook his head, slowly, touching it as if it still hurt. "I made a wish, and then…bam! Here I am."

"Anziano…" I said slowly.

Elder Alsop grabbed my hand and pulled me toward him. We kissed.

It was even better than what had happened yesterday in the van.

"Elder Alsop," I said.

"It's Cliff," he corrected. "What's your real name?"

"It's Jeremy," I returned. I was still holding onto his hand. He smiled.

"Is there anything you need back at the apartment?" he asked.

I shook my head.

"Then let's go to Termini and catch a train somewhere. What do you say?" He looked into my face and I looked carefully into his. All those lost years.

I pulled him back toward me and we kissed again. I took off his name tag and then mine, tossing them onto the sidewalk. "To Oz?" I asked.

He nodded. "To Oz."

Holding hands, we walked the rest of the way to the open market. The 48 pulled up to Piazza Sempione ten minutes later, heading downtown. We each took a deep breath and climbed aboard.

The Gathering 5

When Gavin finished speaking, there was silence in the room, just like after Nellie's story. Had Gavin said something unspeakable? He looked about. He'd never told a living soul he was gay, not even his bishop. He couldn't believe what a relief it was to finally say something.

Had it taken the End of the World to do such a simple thing?

"Gavin," Nellie said coolly, clearly unimpressed by the story. "There's no point airing dirty laundry."

"My laundry's not dirty," he replied.

"I'm sorry," was all Quinn said. Emma just looked at him sadly. She reached over and squeezed his hand. Jon was looking at the floor.

Suddenly, the import of what Nellie had said struck Gavin. "You knew all along?" he asked.

She put her hands on her hips. "I'm not stupid," she replied. "I knew there had to be *some* reason you weren't interested." Then she bit her lip and picked up her embroidery. She pulled out the needle, looked at it as if she didn't know what it was, and stuck it back in the fabric. She set the fabric down.

"I'm sorry, Nellie," he said softly. "Nowadays, they tell people like me to be celibate, but back in the day, they told us to get married."

Nellie took a sip of her water. It still looked like urine.

"But we made it, didn't we, honey?" he asked. "It's almost the Second Coming. We made it."

There was a single, piercing shriek somewhere outside nearby. It lasted a short two seconds and was cut off abruptly.

"That remains to be seen," Nellie said coldly.

"I'm scared," said Quinn.

"What's going to happen when we go to sleep tonight?" asked Emma.

"We'll trust in the Lord," Nellie replied. "Like any good Latter-day Saint would." Jon and Emma looked at each other briefly. Quinn looked at the baby sleeping on the floor.

"It's your turn, Jon," said Gavin. "Tell us a story that makes us feel good."

"A story like mine," said Nellie. "The kind of story we should *all* be telling." She picked up a fresh candle and lit it with the remains of a fading one.

Jon nodded, looked at his watch as if that made any difference in any way to anything, and began his tale.

On the Back of Oxen

Bennett was special, but not special enough to have a vision. At twenty-seven, he was a little young to be called to work in the temple. Retired folks usually received those callings, so much nicer than being called to clean the ward toilet. But he'd told his bishop in no uncertain terms that working as the ward membership clerk, which was only a step above toilet-cleaning on the best of days, was making him lose his testimony. All those people moving in and out of the ward boundaries who insisted they didn't want to be tracked any longer by the Church. It shook his faith.

A month after that discussion, Bennett was called to work the Recommend Desk at the Gilbert Arizona temple. He simply had to sit behind a magnificent mahogany desk in the large square foyer. The room was decorated sparsely but elegantly in brown tones, with a beautiful mosaic on the floor in front of him he could admire his entire shift. No one ever showed up without their credit card recommend, so it was always just a formality to make sure no anti-Mormons were trying to sneak in with recording equipment. By now, the entire endowment ceremony was on YouTube anyway, so it was pretty much a moot point.

Bennett worked just one shift a week, usually the Tuesday 6:00 p.m. to 9:00 p.m. slot. It wasn't a busy time. The last endowment session began at 7:00, so few people came in after that, though baptisms went on till 8:00. There was no cafeteria to direct people to, no clothing rental available. The temple was a magical place in many ways, but it was also a bit mundane. You came and did your service, either as a worker or a patron, and you went home.

And that was the crux of the problem. Bennett didn't have a key, so he couldn't be the last person to leave. Yet he wanted to stay until all the patrons had gone and there were only a few workers left. Maybe then he could find a sacred corner of the building and finally see Jesus. He'd read so many stories of the apostles and prophets, who'd made it all the way to the head of the Church without ever seeing Christ personally, and then finally, one special day in the temple, they'd met face to face. If Bennett were to have any chance at all, it had to be at the end of his shift. It wasn't quite the same thing, but one didn't see ghosts in a busy shopping mall. One saw them in a deserted old house.

"Good night, Brother Alexander," Bennett said softly, waving at an older gentleman on his way out now. Brother Alexander saw him wave and whispered good night in return. Everything was said softly in the temple, at all times. Heavenly Father must simply love golf, Bennett thought.

Brother Alexander worked at the veil. He was so hard of hearing no one ever had any trouble getting through. The man always just assumed he'd heard the patrons incorrectly and ushered them past the checkpoint without correcting them.

Looking at so many elderly people all the time, Bennett worried simultaneously about two things. One, that he'd grow old without ever finding the love of his life. And two, that he'd find the love of his life, and *she'd* grow old and unattractive. It was comforting to know that his wife, or wives, would be eternally young once they reached the

Celestial Kingdom, but he was almost thirty already. That only left him a good ten years before he was middle-aged himself. He'd guarded his chastity all these years, but now he was afraid once he did marry and could freely have sex, his wife would be too old to satisfy him.

Yet even trials like that he could face, even for another thirty or forty years, if only he really *knew*. He simply needed a vision. Perhaps he didn't truly deserve one, not being terribly special in any way, but he wanted one just the same.

Bennett waved good-bye to a few of the other workers, wishing they'd hurry up before he'd be kicked out himself. He had decided this morning on his way to the office downtown that tonight during his temple shift, he was going to have a vision. And by golly, he was going to do it.

The problem was where.

The bathrooms were usually quiet and isolated, but Bennett had determined that wasn't exactly the place he wanted to meet the Redeemer. One of the ordinance rooms where the endowments took place would be too much like a class with its rows and rows of chairs. While Jesus was the Great Teacher, Bennett wanted to meet him on more equal terms. The Celestial Room was an obvious choice, but that sanctuary was closed down at the earliest possible moment, its access restricted even before his shift ended.

It was frustrating trying to find the peace he longed for, when peace was off limits.

What was left? A sealing room? That wouldn't be a bad idea, Bennett thought, but it might spark some awkward questions from the Savior. For instance, why was a righteous

Mormon man still single at his age? Did he not know the importance of marriage? Was he being too picky, thinking himself better than all the daughters of Zion freely available to him in the stake?

No, the sealing room wouldn't do. A reprimand from Jesus wasn't what he was after.

Bennett strolled the halls, carefully, ducking into open doors when the occasional lingering worker passed by. Too many doors were locked at this point. He had to do something quickly. He tried another door. Locked as well.

"Forget something, Brother Benson?"

Bennett swirled around to see Sister Dell looking at him curiously. She helped the elderly sisters put on their caps and aprons at the appropriate points in the ceremony. What she was doing here this late Bennett didn't know.

Did women want to meet the Savior, too?

"Uh, no, I'm fine. Have a good evening." Bennett walked on, remembering just how often people were able to intrude on each other's most personal moments in the temple. Holiness here was a communal experience, whether one wanted it that way or not.

He remembered overhearing two elderly women a couple of weeks ago in the hallway. One of them, still in her temple clothes, turned to the other, who'd just taken off her apron. "You know, when my granddaughter Angie was having so much trouble with her second pregnancy, I came to the temple every single day and put her name on the prayer roll."

"And what happened?" the apronless woman asked.

"Well, naturally, she got better," replied the first woman. "In fact, she didn't have another single problem the rest of her pregnancy."

"Heavenly Father is amazing." She shook her head.

"All it takes is a little faith. I come to the temple once a week now to show my gratitude."

"What a wonderful grandmother you are. Your granddaughter must love you very much."

The women were soon out of range, but the conversation wasn't unusual. The discussion of everyday miracles was another perk of his calling. He'd once heard a man talk about regaining the use of his left hand after a stroke. He heard a woman say she'd lowered her blood pressure by meditating in the Celestial Room, an elderly man say his cancer had gone into remission. Bennett thanked Heavenly Father every night for the privilege of working in this sacred place.

It was just that as wonderful as the environment was, and all the blessings he was already receiving every day, it still wasn't *quite* enough. Joseph Smith had seen God at the age of fourteen. He'd gone on to do a lot of astoundingly great things. That was primarily because he was such a great person to begin with. But there was no denying that seeing God the Father, and Jesus Christ, and Moroni, and Peter, James, and John, and Ezekiel, and all the others simply bestowed an enormous amount of strength on a person.

If only Bennett could see one of these perfect beings.

He peeked in the men's room, knowing it wouldn't be locked yet.

Nothing.

Just as well.

He remembered one time right after attending an endowment session on his own time, he'd gone to the Celestial Room and enjoyed the soothing, peaceful environment. The furnishings were luxurious, the room like the lobby of a five-star hotel. People criticized the Church for spending so much money on temples, but Bennett had seen the cathedrals of northern France during his mission.

Maybe the poor had suffered by their construction, but there was no mistaking the incredible spirit one could feel even in an apostate building, if that building were beautiful. It was only natural that Mormons wanted to experience a little of that in their own places of worship.

But that one night…Bennett closed his eyes, trying to forget. An elderly woman on the sofa next to him had lost control of her bladder, ruining the brocaded fabric. She was mortified and began crying as if her life were over. The attendants talked to her gently and calmed her down as they quietly ushered her out, as comforting as possible.

But during his next shift at the Recommend Desk, Bennett heard one of the other workers tell him the woman's recommend had been revoked.

Rather than go up to the Celestial Room now, which was pointless, Bennett decided to head down to the baptismal font. He'd loved coming to the temple as a teenager and doing baptisms for the dead, the only ordinance teens were allowed to participate in. A line of the youngsters would come from their ward or stake and get dunked fifteen times in a row, hardly having enough time to come up for air before going under the surface of the water again. He'd choked every time. And yet every time he headed back to the dressing room afterwards, dripping wet, he luxuriated in the knowledge that he'd touched eternity.

Bennett paused in the stairwell. This was where he'd overheard the temple president talking to one of the prominent members of the bishopric of his ward one evening. They were on a different level in the stairwell, and Bennett heard them before he saw them.

"Brother Raleigh," the president said, "the best way to deal with wayward children like yours is to cut them out of the will. And I don't just mean your son who's had his name removed from Church records. This goes for your daughter as well. She's active, but she doesn't have a temple recommend any longer." Bennett had slowly descended and could now just see the two men around the corner. He paused, afraid of interrupting such a serious conversation.

"It's such a burden," Brother Raleigh confessed, looking defeated and much older than he'd looked even a few weeks earlier.

"It's money that's a burden," the temple president returned. "And a curse. It's only a blessing in one's life if one is righteous. In the hands of others, it only leads to heartache. Now that you're facing this terrible illness, you need to rewrite your will and leave your money to the Church."

Brother Raleigh looked unhappy, but the temple president noticed Bennett at that point and gave him a withering look, so he had to continue on his way without hearing the rest of the conversation.

Bennett didn't mean to be a peeping Tom. It was just that so many extraordinary things took place in the temple every day. And since it was the temple, those things were often quite personal. It was like accidentally finding you had access to HR's personnel files at the office, when all you were really trying to do was find the photocopier.

But the richness of his experiences scared him. Bennett had decided he needed to start concentrating right away on receiving his vision, realizing he might be released from his calling at any moment. Some people had a given calling for years and years. Other people were released within months. He might not have much longer to see Jesus. And every Tuesday since then, he'd fasted the entire day, hoping to make himself at least slightly more worthy of Christ's presence when he arrived to work his shift.

There were only moments left before Bennett had to leave the building tonight. He descended quietly toward the gallery where the baptisms were performed. The lights would be dimmed but not off. The font itself would be empty by now but this room was almost as spectacular as the Celestial Room. In some ways, spending time in the baptismal chamber was like finding an out-of-the-way eatery in a foreign city, away from the well-traveled avenues, but where the food was so fabulous tour guides would fight over claiming they'd discovered it. Only they never discovered it, which is why it remained such an incredible treasure.

Bennett stopped short when he entered the room. Someone was in the font. In fact, it looked as if there were two people.

In the dim light, Bennett could just make out Brother and Sister Bradford. They always did their shifts together. Married almost sixty years, they did everything together. Bennett had met them at the grocery once wearing matching shirts. That was a harder feat to pull off at church, of course. But they had team taught Gospel Doctrine for years. Brother Bradford had never risen very high in the Church because he'd refused any leadership calling that would force him to spend too much time away from his wife.

Brother Bradford had told him a few weeks ago that he'd meet the girl of his dreams one day and *know* she was right for him. Sister Bradford had said he might even meet her here at the temple. The Bradfords had met each other at the Mesa temple in the Celestial Room decades before. It was sweet of them to worry about his bachelor status, Bennett thought. So many other members made him feel like a failure. These folks made him feel happy, single or not.

Bennett wondered what they were doing in the font. It didn't look like they were cleaning it. In fact, it looked like…

Oh, my heck, thought Bennett. They were having sex. In the temple. On the backs of twelve oxen.

Bennett knew he should turn and walk quietly out of the room, but he was fascinated by the sight in front of him. He'd never been the kind to look at pornography. He didn't even allow himself to watch R-rated movies. The fact that he had access to the temple proved he'd passed his temple recommend interviews regularly.

But he did *think* about sex sometimes. He watched as Brother Bradford pulled backward and pushed forward, pumping his groin toward his wife. They were both fully dressed from the top up, just in white, no temple accessories visible. Bennett couldn't see anything down below, and given their age, he decided that was probably a good thing.

Bennett had no idea how long they'd been at it before he showed up, but the sex seemed to go on forever, slowly, methodically, for another ten minutes. Neither of them seemed to feel any great passion, but when they finally finished, Brother Bradford leaned forward and softly kissed his wife on the lips.

They zipped up or pulled up and fastened whatever they were wearing down below, and that might have been the end of that. But then Brother Bradford took his wife in his arms and made the motion of baptizing her, even though there was no water in the font. Bennett's brows furrowed in confusion. But it was what happened next that most surprised him. Sister Bradford then took her husband in her arms and baptized him as well.

Afterward, they climbed out of the font and headed toward another exit. They hadn't seen him at all.

Bennett was tingling all over. He wondered if the feeling was the witness of the Holy Ghost. He'd felt something similar when he watched the film about the First Vision.

Of course, he'd also had this feeling when watching a particularly moving story on the Hallmark channel. So who knew?

Bennett looked about carefully and then walked hesitantly to the middle of the room. He climbed the steps leading to the font, looked around again, and stepped slowly inside. He turned around and looked at the columns and curtains and chandeliers and everything else in the room. So very beautiful.

And he felt as if he were standing waist deep in love.

Had he witnessed a proxy honeymoon? He'd never seen anything so lovely.

Surely, this was the night Bennett was going to meet the Savior. He wanted to close his eyes in prayer, but he was afraid he'd miss the vision. "Heavenly Father," he whispered, the words sounding loud in the silence, "I believe you're real. I…I *know* you are. But I know I could do something truly great with my life if you just showed yourself." He shook his head. "Not you personally, of course. I know only very special people get to see *you*. But I really want to see Jesus, know my Savior. If you could—"

"Hey!" someone shouted from the doorway. "What are you doing in there?"

Bennett turned to see Brother Flake. The guy with the keys. Speaking in a much louder tone than usual in the building. "I…I…"

"Get out of there right now. I've got to lock up." He shook his head in disgust as Bennett climbed out of the font and walked sheepishly toward him. "You newbies drive me crazy." He patted Bennett on the back as they headed back into the hallway. "Don't worry, though. You'll get over it."

Brother Flake ushered Bennett out of the building, though he stayed inside himself. Was *he* trying to see Jesus, Bennett wondered?

As he inserted his key into the door of his car, Bennett looked across the parking lot and watched as Brother Bradford two rows over held the car door of his own vehicle open for his wife before climbing into the driver's seat a moment later. The taillights came on, and the car backed slowly out of its spot. It turned and rolled smoothly toward the gate.

Bennett looked up into the night sky, only a few stars visible over the lights of the parking lot and the town around them. He'd so wanted to see a vision tonight.

He sat in his car and turned on some classical music, the same as he did every night after his Tuesday shift. He started the engine and pulled out into the street, heading home. Work would start again early in the morning.

But not before he faced eight hours alone in an empty apartment.

Handel's water music played around him, and Bennett closed his eyes tightly at a stoplight. All he could see was an old couple making love in an empty font.

But then Veronica's face came to him. She was a full year older than he was and had a five-year-old daughter by a man she'd never married. But she always talked for fifteen minutes every week after Sacrament meeting to the nearly deaf widow everyone else ignored.

The light turned green and a car honked behind him. Bennett stepped on the gas and drove on.

The Gathering 6

"Oh, for pity's sake," Nellie said, "does everyone have to talk about sex?" She shook her head in disgust. "You'd think we were all watching HBO or Showtime." She looked at Gavin. "Something *we* certainly never subscribed to."

"I'm sorry," said Jon, and he sounded sincere. "I guess living this close to death, everyone must be experiencing primal feelings."

"Well, take a cold shower while we still have water," said Nellie. "For pity's sake."

"Look, it's late," said Gavin. "We really should all get to bed. Christ won't be coming back tonight." He thought for a second. "Isn't he supposed to come back during the day?"

"It's always day somewhere," Quinn pointed out.

"So what are the sleeping arrangements?" asked Emma. "I mean, it's a big, dark house. And there are boogeymen outside." She forced a chuckle.

"Nellie and I share the master bedroom, of course," Gavin said, "but there are three other bedrooms. Plenty of room for everyone."

"Harper and I will take the bedroom farthest away," Quinn decided, "in case she wakes up in the night. You guys have enough on your minds without listening to that."

Nobody disagreed.

"You look exhausted, too," said Emma. She paused a moment and then turned to Nellie. "You guys didn't save a year's supply of alcohol, did you? You know, for medicinal purposes?"

Nellie looked at Emma with repulsion. "Certainly not."

Emma turned to Quinn. "It was worth a shot," she said.

"Any Nyquil or anything?" asked Quinn. "I wouldn't give her much. She's so tiny. But it's not only a matter of a good night's sleep for me and everyone else. It'll be safer, too, if no one out there hears noises inside the house."

At this, Nellie frowned. She looked over at the sleeping baby and thought for a moment. Finally, she said, "I'll show you the Nyquil." She picked up a candle and led Quinn down the hallway.

Emma turned to Jon. "I'm afraid to sleep by myself."

Jon smiled slyly. "I'm not very strong if anyone breaks in."

"You're better than nothing."

He grinned in embarrassment. "Shall we put that on my tombstone?"

Emma shook her head. "You're never going to need a tombstone. You're going to live into the Millennium and be resurrected instantly when you turn seventy-six."

"I'll show you guys to your room," said Gavin. "For heaven's sake, don't tell Nellie you're sharing."

They passed the bathroom, where Gavin lit a new candle to burn throughout the night before directing Emma and Jon to Peter's old room. Gavin paused, hoping Peter and his family were okay. And the girls and their families, too.

Or maybe it was better if they were all dead. No more worry and fear and torment.

What kind of faith told people death was better than life?

"Good night, Gavin," Emma said. She took Jon's arm and led him into the bedroom, closing the door behind them.

Gavin continued on to the master bedroom, where he stripped down to his garments. He fingered the embroidered symbols a moment and then slid into bed. Maybe it wouldn't be the worst thing in the world if someone broke in tonight and killed him. Better to die now than fall into sin just hours before the Second Coming. His faith did tell him that was what he should believe.

He thought about Jon and felt a stiffening in his groin.

He forced himself to think of Nellie and soon grew flaccid again. A few minutes later, Nellie joined him in bed. "Night, honey," he said softly.

"Whatever," she replied. Then she blew out the candle.

The Gathering 7

Nellie was no longer in the bed when Gavin woke up. He reached over and felt the sheets. Cold. She'd been up for a while. It was sunny, a relief to see light streaming through the curtains after so many hours in near or total darkness.

He sure didn't want to end up in Outer Darkness. He needed to hang on a little longer. He knelt beside the bed and prayed for strength. Or for death in lieu of strength.

Gavin went to the bathroom and emptied both his bladder and his bowels, breathing in relief to discover the toilet still flushed. Then he joined Nellie in the kitchen. She was cooking some freeze-dried strips of bacon on the stove. "May as well cook while I can," she said. "There's nothing fresh left, but heated is still better than cold."

Gavin kissed her on the back of the neck.

"Don't even think about it, mister," she said. "I'm not forgetting what you said last night."

"I love you, Nellie," he replied. "I wouldn't be with you all this time if I didn't." He wondered if it was true.

She didn't reply but started filling the rainbow glasses with water again. Soon everyone was seated around the kitchen table. Quinn put the baby down on some blankets in the living room. "I've already fed her," she said. "Thank you for storing all that formula."

"We obey the Lord," Nellie said.

"Jon," said Gavin, "would you ask a blessing on the food?" He saw Jon and Emma exchange a brief smile.

After the prayer, they all began to eat. The food really wasn't very good, but no one offered a word of complaint. They all brushed their teeth, washed up, and headed to the living room. Quinn pulled back the curtain a few inches to peer outside. The mid-morning sun shone through.

"It looks quiet," she said.

"Feel free to go out if you like," said Nellie without looking up. She was embroidering her runner again.

Everyone sat in their same spots from the evening before. "No Bugs Bunny on TV yet, I take it," said Jon, "so perhaps we should pick up where we left off last night." He grinned at Emma. "'For some must push and some must pull,'" he sang off key. Emma blushed.

"Who wants to go first?" asked Gavin. He dreaded his own turn later. God only knew what he was going to say.

"Me," said Quinn. She was holding the baby, making the infant grab one of her fingers, and then pretending she couldn't get free. "Taking a shower this morning made me remember a time I went swimming in a lake." She paused. "Without a bathing suit."

"Do tell," said Jon, laughing. Emma gave him the evil eye.

"You're not going to talk about sex again, are you?" asked Nellie, shaking her head. "Why the Lord spared you guys I'll never know." She stabbed her needle into the fabric. Then she looked up in surprise, an expression of wonder on her face. "Maybe it was to test me," she breathed. "Because Heavenly Father knew that just the Apocalypse alone wasn't enough for someone like me." She nodded in comprehension while everyone else looked at each other stupefied, trying not to laugh.

It was going to be a long day, thought Gavin. He leaned back in his recliner and listened to Quinn tell her story.

The Three Nephites Go Skinny-dipping

A naked man was slowly climbing up out of the lake, water clinging to his skin as if too aroused to let go. He joined two other nude men sitting on towels nearby. They seemed oblivious to the possibility of being seen by any other vacationers. Their long, flaccid penises proclaimed their innocence in the freedom of the outdoors.

I swatted at a mosquito and thought about blood supply.

I was twenty-two and had just graduated from Brigham Young University with a degree in Economics. Regular economics, not the Home kind. As a result, I had no marriage prospects and was debating going straight on to grad school or taking eighteen months off to serve a mission. I thought it might be good to work in South America and learn Spanish fluently while discovering another culture. If I didn't pass my temple recommend interview, serving in the Peace Corps was also an option. And if I found I didn't have the commitment to do either, I was pretty handy with a hammer and could always help Habitat for Humanity on weekends.

Especially Sundays.

I'd tried to get my endowments while at BYU, and although I never officially broke the Honor Code, my student ward leaders always dissuaded me from going to the temple. "Susan, that's a special experience that should wait until marriage," one bishop told me, "though we can certainly make a concession if you insist on serving a mission. But a woman's primary calling is always to be a wife and mother."

Since I hadn't wanted to interrupt my education with either children or missionary companions, I never went to the temple. Still, I wore white T-shirts underneath my blouses so that people straining to see if I was worthy wouldn't be able to tell if I was wearing garments or not. I thought about having my sister buy me a few pairs of the real thing, but I knew she'd be horrified at the suggestion. Then I thought about stealing a pair of hers when I went to visit, but breaking one of the Ten Commandments seemed an awkward way to feel holy.

Of course, ordering young men and women to repress themselves sexually during their prime years seemed like the perfect recipe for sin, so maybe I didn't really understand righteousness very well. If the Church was moaning about so many of its members being "addicted" to pornography, perhaps it shouldn't leave porn as the only available option for release.

But I was an A student, so I wasn't stupid enough to ever such a thing in public. Now that I had my diploma and transcripts, I thought I'd do my graduate work at the University of Utah, where if I confessed to heavy petting, I wouldn't be banned from classes.

Why the heck did I need to confess in any case?

As a graduation treat to myself, I drove across Nevada to stay a few days in Lake Tahoe. The scenery was breathtaking, though the lake was lower than it had been in ages because of the drought, making the beach much wider than it had been in recorded history. And it was on this beach where the three naked men were lying in the sun.

Standing up the trail hidden by bushes, I felt like a voyeur, so I decided to continue with my original plan and walked on down to the lake.

"Hi, guys," I said. "How's the water?"

One of the men jumped to his feet, but the other two remained on their backs. "It's perfect," said the man who was standing, making no effort to conceal his member. Not that he would have been able to. "I see you're Mormon."

I stopped and looked at him in surprise. "And just how did you determine that?" I demanded.

"The one-piece bathing suit." He smiled. "And, of course, your sweet spirit."

"Oh." I set my towel and Deseret romance down and continued to the water's edge, dipping my toes in the water. "A little cool," I said.

"It starts to feel warm quickly," the man returned.

"The water's getting warmer everywhere these days," one of the other men said. He spread his legs a little wider.

"You go swimming a lot?" I asked, stepping farther into the water, letting it cover my ankles.

"Every chance we get," said the man who was standing. All three men had dark brown hair, almost black. They had the same olive skin and high cheekbones, too, probably brothers or cousins. All three were reasonably fit without being either too slender or too muscular, a Goldilocks combination of features. The only real way to tell them apart was by their penises. Standing Man's penis hung halfway down to his knees, it seemed. Lying Man One's penis was maybe seven or eight inches long with a much larger girth than Standing Man's, and Lying Man Two's penis was almost the same length as Lying Man One's, judging from this distance, but so sharply curved that it almost looked broken.

"See anything you like?" asked Lying Man One.

"Just making a mental note in case I have to talk to the police later," I said.

The three men chuckled. "Honey," said Lying Man Two, "we are so over sex these days even someone as modestly dressed as you isn't very tempting."

I frowned.

"You guys can't be over thirty," I said, "and you've already had so much sex you're sick of it?" I had to admit that, as a virgin, the idea of ever being satiated seemed mystifying. I walked deeper into the lake until the water almost reached my knees.

"I reached a hundred thousand orgasms several years ago," said Lying Man One. Standing Man looked at him sternly, which seemed to have no effect. Lying Man One flipped his penis from the right to the left. It remained flaccid.

"Was there a ticker tape parade?" I asked. The number he proposed was clearly nonsense.

Lying Man Two stood up and pointed to his crotch. "Mine broke at twenty thousand," he said. "This woman was trying to sit on me and—"

"Oh, for goodness' sake," said Standing Man. "Are you going to tell the poor woman in detail every single one of your sexual encounters?"

"It helps pass the time," he replied. "And time sure does go by slowly some days."

I stepped deeper into the lake until the water came halfway up my thighs. "Did you guys escape from somewhere?" I asked. "Some place that makes you wear distinctive clothing you had to ditch?"

Lying Man One laughed. Lying Man Two picked up a book and started to read. Standing Man reached into a blue cooler and grabbed a Coke in a glass bottle. "Mexi-Coke," he said, taking a swig. "There's nothing better. Want one?"

Despite what the guys had said, the water was not getting the least bit warmer, and since all three men were still limp, I felt I could risk going nearer. I stepped back up onto the beach and walked over to them. "I'd love one," I said. Standing Man opened a bottle and handed it to me. I swigged half the contents in one draw. Lying Man One clapped. Standing Man raised his bottle in salute.

"So what's your story, guys?" I asked.

"Before I answer," said Lying Man One, "let me ask you a question."

I shrugged.

"Have you ever sat in Sacrament meeting and thought, 'Oh, my god, if I hear just one more lame talk on that same asinine subject, I'll go crazy'?"

I frowned again, looking at each man in turn. Something funny was going on. "Everyone feels that way," I answered.

"Well, let me tell you," Lying Man One continued, "I've been teaching the same lesson day after day, week after week, month after month, year after year..." He took a breath. "...century after century. And goddamn if I'm not tired of hearing myself talk."

"You're not the only one," Lying Man Two muttered.

"Fuck you."

I stepped farther back.

Standing Man took another sip of his Coke and shrugged. "It's no great secret at this point," he said. "Surely, you've figured out by now we're the Three Nephites."

I laughed, surprised not to be feeling the fear I should have been experiencing. "But I don't have a flat tire," I pointed out.

Now it was their turn to laugh. "Changing tires gets old, too," Lying Man One admitted.

Now that the conversation was going in this new direction, Lying Man Two put his book down. "Oh, for crying out loud," he said in disgust, "all this pussyfooting around gets tiresome as well. Enough with the flirting. Just ask the woman already."

Standing Man and Lying Man One looked at each other for a moment, and then Standing Man took a last sip from his bottle. I could see where this was going and had to work hard to keep myself from smiling at their transparency. These must be BYU grad students on vacation. The stories I'd heard other women at the Y tell about predatory male students were legion. And the Three Nephite angle kind of made sense.

It was sort of like the economic theory proposed by John Nash. If a guy approached one woman and she turned him down, he couldn't very well approach the woman's friends next. Something like that. These men must have figured that the best way for any one of them to score was to do it as a team.

"I'm a virgin," I said, "and I plan to stay that way until I'm married in the temple." They didn't need to know that I had a vibrator back home.

"You'll never find a more experienced man," said Lying Man One. "Or men."

"Yeah," I said drily, "it's a tempting offer, but I'll pass."

"It has nothing to do with temptation," said Standing Man. "When Jesus changed our bodies so we could stay alive until his return, he didn't stop our bodies from producing testosterone."

Lying Man Two groaned. "You had to go there, didn't you? You had to start talking about our resurrected testicles."

"They're not resurrected," Standing Man countered. "We're still mortal until we get changed in the twinkling of an eye at the beginning of the Millennium."

"May as well be resurrected for all the difference it makes," Lying Man Two said.

"Your penis won't be broken any more once we're really resurrected."

"You guys!" I said, laughing. "You've got this schtick down pat. It's incredible!" I drank the last half of my Coke in one long guzzle.

"Where I was going before I was interrupted," Standing Man said, "was that it isn't a sin to serve God's servants. It's like members of the Church feeding the missionaries. Celibacy for a lifetime is one thing, and that's hard enough. But celibacy for ten lifetimes? Twenty? Even Heavenly Father isn't that cruel."

"But you guys just said you were sick and tired of sex."

Standing Man shrugged. "You get sick of Sacrament meeting, but you still go." He looked at his two friends and then back at me. "And that isn't even driven by hormones."

I set my empty bottle beside the cooler and took another look at the three men. On the one hand, my own hormones were raging rather abundantly, and I wasn't even dating anyone seriously right now. There was no telling how long it would be before I was legally married and free to do what I'd fantasized about for years. And the men were in fact rather attractive.

No one would know I'd committed this sin, so there'd really be no lasting repercussions. I'd have had at least one real adventure in my life, sex with three strangers at one time. If their preposterous claim was true, then the adventure was all the more exciting. And despite knowing how ridiculous their assertions were, I had to admit I routinely believed a lot of things even more unlikely. So why couldn't this be real as well?

On the other hand…

"You guys have condoms?" I asked. "I don't need any sperm donors."

"And we sure don't need any more kids," said Lying Man Two. "How Heavenly Father keeps up with billions I'll never know."

Standing Man kneeled beside his towel and opened a fanny pack. He pulled out a strip of condoms and a bottle of lubricant.

"I see you're Boy Scouts as well."

"We're the ones who gave them their motto to begin with," said Lying Man One. "Who knows more about living in the wilderness?"

"Though we spend most of our time in Reno these days."

I nodded and began peeling off my suit. The men didn't look all that interested, even after I lay down on Standing Man's towel. I wasn't sure I felt very aroused myself, perhaps because of all the limp penises. The Lying Men continued to lie down and watched almost in boredom as Standing Man bathed some lubricant on his penis until it finally responded and then slipped on his condom. "I hate these things," he said.

I shrugged.

"You sure we need it?" he persisted. "We could just soak if you don't want to go all the way."

He saw my look and left it on.

I'd say it was all over with the three men in fifteen minutes, but it took almost ninety. Despite their claims of being driven by hormones, it seemed almost a Herculean effort on their part to reach climax. At least a Sisyphean one. Hardly the thing to get me wet, so I was grateful for the lube. They did at least come, though, which was more than I managed.

You'd think they'd have learned a useful technique or two in all those years, whether it was a mere ten or a full two thousand, but I suppose that would have required seeing their sexual partners as equals worthy of attention. I picked up Lying Man Two's novel and started reading before he finished. His final thrust knocked the book out of my hand. And I was right in the middle of a sentence. He groaned and said, "When ye are in the service of your fellow man, ye are only in the service of your god."

"It was good for me, too," I said. As he rolled off, I turned to Standing Man. "Got another Mexi-Coke?"

We all sat there on the beach, swigging our Cokes silently, looking out on the shrinking lake. Finally, I mustered the courage to ask the one question that needed to be asked, even if it was just to humor them. "Do you know how much longer we have to wait?" If ninety minutes could seem like a long time, I couldn't imagine waiting for centuries.

"No man knows the day or the hour," Standing Man said reverently.

"Yes, but the scriptures don't say no one knows the year."

The three men looked at each other. Standing Man shrugged. "We still have a lot more Sacrament meetings to attend," was all he said. His companions looked down at the ground unhappily.

I stood up and pulled my swimsuit back on. I took another Mexi-Coke for the hike back and waved goodbye. I was determined to experience my first orgasm with another living person today and thought about the desk clerk back at the hotel. I wished I had some garments I could flash a little to entice him. The Three Nephites waved back listlessly and then lay down on their towels again. Lying Man Two picked up his book. I guzzled half my Coke in one draw and started walking.

The Gathering 8

"Well, that was an absolutely revolting story," said Nellie in Quinn's general direction. "You know, it's not as if I can't kick you out, just because I let you in. You had better repent and get closer to Heavenly Father and Jesus Christ while you can."

"Then you won't get the temptation you need," Emma pointed out. "To prove how much better than the rest of us you are."

Nellie gave her an icy stare. "Don't think I won't do it."

"Now, now," said Gavin. "There's no need to get at each other's throats."

"The people outside will do that for us soon enough," Jon reminded everyone. Now Gavin was the one to issue an icy stare.

"You seem to be enjoying all the talk about sex," Emma said tightly to Jon, adding her own icy stare. The room was definitely cooling off.

Jon shrugged. "It's kind of like pioneer days, isn't it?" he said. "Not enough men to go around. It's why we had polygamy in the first place."

Quinn snorted. "Is that why Joseph married other men's wives?"

"They were away on missions," Jon said defensively. "It's just like Eric not being here now. I'm available to help Emma and he's not."

"You're such an asshole."

"That's not what you told me last night when I was 'helping' you."

Nellie looked from one to the other and then at Gavin with an accusing stare. Perhaps she was right. This was all his fault.

Everything was always his fault.

"I want to tell a story," Emma said, sitting forward in her seat. "About facing Judgment Day."

"Oh, brother," Quinn muttered.

"Exactly the kind of story we should be telling," Nellie agreed, taking a sip from her yellow cup. Gavin could almost smell the urinal at the office. Where he'd lingered some days, hoping to see a fellow worker's penis, but even when another man was standing beside him, he could never bring himself to look.

No matter what anyone else did or didn't do, he had to stay strong. If he alone passed the test of Earth life, then so be it. If these stories helped in the slightest, he would go along.

Emma stuck her tongue out at Jon and began.

Plane Crash on Kolob

"You're sixteen years old," said Jeanette. "Don't you ever want to date?" Jeanette herself even wanted to go out with non-members, but her father forbid it.

Kesley laughed. "Babysitting for my neighbors is fun," she replied. "And what's the point of dating anyway?" She glanced across the room at Josh. "I still have to go on a mission when I turn nineteen. No point getting involved now."

"But you're not even being paid," Jeanette persisted. "It's…it's…unhealthy."

Kesley smiled. "Oh, Jeanette," she said, "I'm getting paid in ways so much better than money. I get to practice being a mother. I get to serve others. And I even get to teach the kids a little about the gospel."

Jeanette made an effort not to roll her eyes. "Your neighbors don't mind you brainwashing their children?"

"It's not brainwashing. It's teaching the truth. And since I'm babysitting for free, they don't make many demands."

"I can imagine." Jeanette turned away from Kesley and joined her friends Shauna and Naomi in another part of the meetinghouse foyer. All the youth in their Walnut Creek ward were gathered for a special fireside. They'd been told about it for weeks, but no one knew what the topic was going to be. Probably chastity or the dangers of watching inappropriate television. Then this morning in church, all the kids were given an envelope. When Jeanette opened hers, she found a plane ticket. The destination was Salt Lake City. She'd groaned. But there was no way to avoid coming back this evening. With the bishop as her father, she was always expected to be a "good girl."

She looked about the foyer now. All the kids were holding plane tickets. Josh and Kesley were talking by the chapel doors. He was on track to be Valedictorian when he graduated from high school in a couple of months. Cary, David, and Tony were deacons, earning new merit badges every month in Scouting, but still reprimanded for chewing gum during Sacrament meeting. And then of course there were her best friends, Shauna and Naomi.

They were both MIA Maids while she was a Laurel, but they were far more interesting to hang out with than her fellow classmate Kesley, that was for sure. Shauna liked skateboarding and Naomi liked playing the guitar. Jeanette fantasized about the three of them forming a band sometime. Only Shauna couldn't sing, and Jeanette could only play treble clef on the piano. She'd quit her lessons back when she was eight.

"If I'm old enough to know right from wrong and be baptized," she'd told her parents at the time, "then I'm old enough to know I don't want to play the piano."

She smiled at the memory. Her teachers at school had always said she was unusually precocious, and even now, they complained she was bright enough to be earning straight A's, but schoolwork bored her. She wanted to become a professional tennis player.

"Okay, everyone," said Sister Gerard, the Laurel instructor, clapping her hands. She looked disappointed more kids hadn't shown up. Not that there were that many more in the ward who were active. But what kid wanted to spend their Sunday evening at church when they only had a few more hours of freedom left before going back to school on Monday? Jeanette thought Sister Gerard should be grateful the attendance was as high as it was.

"It's time to go into the gym." Sister Gerard ushered everyone through the doors leading to the Cultural Hall.

Jeanette followed the others and found the basketball court set up with a few rows of chairs and a magazine rack with copies of *The Ensign*, *The New Era*, and *LDS Living*. There were copies of the *Deseret News* newspaper as well. What in the world was everyone up to? Jeanette heard a voice over a loudspeaker. Rather, it sounded like a recording of a voice pretending to come over a loudspeaker. "Will the Clawsons meet their party at the information desk?" the monotone female voice said. It sounded like one of the Primary teachers. Sister Cortez maybe? As the kids moved over to the chairs, the voice continued. "There has been a gate change for passengers on flight 262 to Nauvoo. Please go to Gate Six to board your plane."

Sister Gerard had left them all in the gym by themselves. No adults were present. Jeanette looked at her ticket. She was on flight 1212. She pointed to the chairs, and she, Shauna, and Naomi sat down. The deacons tore a couple of pages out of the newspaper and made paper airplanes. Kesley and Josh opened their scriptures and pointed out verses to each other.

Jeanette rolled her eyes. She couldn't help it this time.

"Where's the Starbucks?" Jeanette called out, hoping one of the adults lurking in the hallway would hear.

Shauna and Naomi giggled. "You're so bad, Jeanette!" Shauna said. Jeanette smiled in return.

Soft, light music played on the recording in between announcements. Jeanette and her friends chatted a few moments until the next important announcement was made. "Flight 1212 is now boarding at Gate Four. Flight 1212 is now boarding at Gate Four." Sister Buchanan, the Seminary instructor, appeared over by the stairway leading up to the stage and waved everyone over. As the kids filed past, she tore off the stubs on their tickets and guided them up the steps.

The curtains were closed, so Jeanette hadn't been able to see the stage from the gym floor. But now she saw that there were four rows of chairs, three on one side of an aisle and two on the other. This was to be their plane. Jeanette grabbed Shauna and Naomi and quickly sat in the front row on the left. "We're first class!" she shouted. "I want some champagne!"

The other kids sat down as well, and Sister Gerard showed up again, now acting as a flight attendant. Jeanette had no idea where all this was leading, but it was certainly more interesting than most of the firesides she was forced to attend. She'd be finished her junior year in high school soon, and then had only one more year before college. Her father insisted she attend Brigham Young University, but that was the last place Jeanette wanted to go. She didn't really want to go to college at all, but if she had to, someplace like Berkeley would be better.

Sister Gerard stood in front of the group, in the aisle at the front of the plane, and gave everyone the emergency directions. The voice of Brother Hamilton, the first counselor in the bishopric, played on the recording. "Stand by for takeoff," he said. Then there was the sound of plane engines revving up and a plane rushing down the runway.

"This is so fun!" Naomi whispered.

Jeanette turned to look behind her. The deacons were in the row behind them, an empty chair between each of them. They were flying the paper airplanes back and forth to each other. Josh and Kesley were in the back seat on the right, pretending to peer out the plane's window, while all they were really looking at was the curtain.

"Miss? Oh, Miss?" said Jeanette, trying to catch Sister Gerard's attention. "Where's the lavatory?"

Sister Gerard kept a professional smile on her face, but Jeanette could see the irritation in her eyes. The woman would be reporting to Jeanette's father about her behavior later, and Jeanette would probably be grounded. Again. But even when she was forbidden to use her phone or computer, there were always books to read. She was finishing one now about Martina Navratilova. And she could always practice her swing in the bedroom with her racket.

Sister Gerard grabbed a cart, one of those the teachers usually put a TV on when they wanted to show a film in class. She pushed it slowly down the aisle, handing out small packets of peanuts.

"Uh, Miss?" said Jeanette. "I think it's against airline policy to hand out peanuts. Someone may be allergic. Peanut dust gets in the air."

Shauna smothered a laugh, and Sister Gerard pretended not to hear what Jeanette had said. A few minutes later, she went back up the aisle with her cart, handing out cans of 7-Up. Jeanette thought about making another smart remark, but she didn't want to be an ass.

Suddenly, there was a loud explosion and bright red lights flashed about the stage. All the kids froze in their seats, peanuts or soda halfway to their lips, as they tried to figure out what had just happened. The lights went out for a moment, the deacons yelled, and then the lights came back on but dimmer than before. Another voice came on the recording. It was her father.

"Flight 1212 has just crashed," he said solemnly. "There were no survivors."

Shauna grasped Jeanette's hand tightly, and Jeanette frowned. Didn't the girl realize this was all pretend? There was nothing to get upset about. She wasn't actually dead. Sheesh.

"You will now all go to the Spirit World. Please follow your guide."

Sister Buchanan reappeared wearing a white dress. She motioned for all the kids to stand up. "Please follow me," she said softly. "No talking, please." They exited through the rear of the plane, Kesley and Josh leading, the deacons next, and Jeanette and her friends trailing behind. Shauna was still grasping onto her hand tightly.

"What do you think—" Naomi began, but Sister Buchanan turned around with her finger to her lips, and Naomi stopped speaking.

They walked off the stage and down the hallway to the Relief Society room, all taking seats on the front row. Soft music played. Before the ban on speaking became too hard to maintain, Brother Hamilton entered the room, also wearing white. "Your lives have been reviewed," he said, "and you've been assigned to the degree of glory you've earned." He paused to let the import of what he'd just said sink in. Jeanette could pretty well figure out where this was going. She turned to Shauna and rolled her eyes. But Shauna looked as if she'd just witnessed a mugging.

"I'll call out three groups. Please stand with your group and follow your angel to your kingdom," Brother Hamilton continued. "Josh and Kesley, please form group one." He smiled at them beatifically, which Jeanette thought made him look like a pervert, and the two young royals stood off to the side. "Cary, David, and Tony, please form group two." The boys clapped each other on the back and moved to the other side of the room. Then Bishop Hamilton looked forlornly at the three remaining girls. Jeanette wanted to slap him for making such a show of their judgment. "Naomi, Shauna, and Jeanette," he said, "you girls will form group three."

Sister Gerard showed up in white to lead group one away and Sister Moss showed up in white to lead group two away. She was the Beehive instructor, and none of her students had come to the fireside tonight. Jeanette wanted to stick out her tongue in vindication. But Shauna was still squeezing her fingers so hard she thought she might lose circulation.

Sister Anderson arrived dressed in white and motioned for group three to follow her. She was the ward organist, the best the ward could manage though the woman still hit two wrong notes for every ten correct ones. Jeanette and her friends followed down the hallway. She saw group two enter the High Council room and could only assume group one was headed for the chapel. She followed Sister Anderson to the Nursery. Jeanette gritted her teeth. She might be a C student, but she was smart enough to understand symbolism.

Sister Anderson closed the Nursery door behind them and motioned for the girls to sit in the tiny seats. Brother Anderson was already waiting for them, also dressed in white. Jeanette couldn't wait for this horrible ordeal to be over. Close to an hour must have passed since they'd started the fireside. It couldn't last much longer. If her father grounded her again, she would insist that include skipping church. "Making me miss services is the greatest punishment you can give me," she'd say. "Since it's the most important event of the week." She'd have to eliminate any trace of sarcasm from her voice and need to start practicing as soon as she got home.

Brother Anderson raised his hand and cleared his throat. "Young women," he began, "you're here today in the Telestial Kingdom because you have not been stalwart members of the Church. You had the gospel your entire lives and chose to waste the precious gift you were given. You are to spend eternity here without your families, forever single. You'll live the rest of your existence with liars and fornicators and murderers. People who drank and smoked. Hitler and serial killers and prostitutes will be your neighbors."

The temptation was too much. While Shauna and Naomi looked as if they'd just been told their noses would fall off from leprosy, Jeanette simply *had* to say something. "And will alcohol be served now?" she asked. "I want a beer."

Shauna and Naomi gasped. Jeanette had been hoping for a laugh. But Brother Anderson smiled. And yet there was something incredibly creepy about the way he was looking at her. Sister Anderson walked over to him and handed him an envelope, which he opened ceremoniously.

"It looks like there's been an error in assignment," he said, looking at the letter in his hands.

Shauna squeezed Jeanette's fingers again.

"Jeanette, will you follow your guide?" Brother Anderson pointed to his wife, and Jeanette followed her out of the room. When she looked behind at the doorway, she saw her friends looking at her as if she were on her way to the guillotine. She was a little confused now, but whatever was about to happen, it wouldn't be good. She followed Sister Anderson down the hallway.

They reached the girls' bathroom, and Sister Anderson opened the door to let Jeanette pass in ahead of her. The air was filled with some kind of pungent incense, almost nauseating. Standing at the sink was her father, dressed in white. Jeanette felt her face burning.

"Jeanette," her father said, "you've been cast into Outer Darkness. You were a valiant spirit in the Pre-Existence and given to a wonderful family on Earth. But you squandered away your blessings and deliberately chose to walk an evil path. You will spend eternity in the dark with Satan and his followers." He paused, and Jeanette felt as if she'd been whipped with a belt, even though her father hadn't done that in years. "If only you had repented while you were alive. You could still have had a future in the Celestial Kingdom."

He turned on a CD player, and loud, heavy metal music filled the air. He and Sister Anderson headed for the door, and as they left, Jeanette's father turned off the light switch. Jeanette stood in the blackness of the bathroom, her ears pounding from the blast of the awful music.

She was livid. She ran over in her mind her non-Mormon friends from school, wondering if any of them had parents who would let her live with them. She thought about thanking her father for introducing her to a fantastic new band. She wanted to get a second and third piercing in her ears. She wondered if she should go to BYU and make it through three years before deliberately breaking the Honor Code and being expelled without her transcripts, wasting years and years of her father's tuition money.

Outer Darkness. Who did he think he was kidding?

Jeanette knew she could walk over to the light switch and turn it back on. She knew she could click off the CD player. She knew once she graduated high school, she could move out and never see her parents again. She knew she could go home tonight and tell her father just how preposterous the whole evening had been.

But instead, she sat down on the cold, tile floor and cried.

The Gathering 9

"Well, thank goodness," said Nellie, putting down her embroidery and clapping politely as if she were at the opera, "finally, someone has told a good story."

Gavin and Quinn exchanged glances, though Gavin kept his face blank.

"Yes, Emma, that was very inspiring," Jon said. Gavin couldn't read his expression. Jon seemed to be learning.

"Everyone is always trying to be so PC," Nellie continued. "Always afraid of hurting weak people's feelings." She shook her head. "But you know, sometimes the truth hurts. If you don't live your life the way you're supposed to, there are consequences."

Gavin thought about what Jon and Emma had done the night before. He'd felt, even as he led them to the same bedroom, that they were sinning, and that it was ridiculous to do such a thing only days away from the end of their test. But at the same time, he'd wondered if perhaps doing something wild and crazy was exactly the right thing to do in circumstances like this. And then he wondered if trying to offer one another some small degree of comfort and companionship was something that could truly be classified as "wild and crazy" in the first place.

What if the only way for Emma to cope with the sudden loss of her husband and children was to do something others thought both decadent and appallingly insensitive?

Gavin shook his head. He wondered if he really even wanted to become a god some day in the distant future. Judging a planet full of his own spirit children just seemed too horrific a task. But then, Jesus was supposed to be the Judge, not Heavenly Father. Perhaps Gavin would be able to foist the task off on someone else as well.

Celestial delegation of the dirty work.

The Atonement had been no fun task, either, Gavin was sure.

Quinn took a sip of water from her green plastic glass and then sniffed the air. Her nose led her to the baby, and she moved off a few feet to change another diaper. When she came back from depositing the used one out back, she said, "Lots of haze outside. Smells smoky out there."

"Surely, the bad guys are going to die off soon," Jon said, looking encouragingly at Emma.

"Well, there was another pretty bad smell out there," Quinn admitted. "Like a dead dog in the street."

"That probably wasn't a dog," said Gavin.

No one knew how to respond to that. Nellie looked especially pensive and was the first to find something to say a few minutes later. "Even though there are lots of jack-Mormons in Hurricane, there are enough people here with food storage to keep a gang of marauders alive for quite some time."

Gavin looked in the corner to make sure his rifle was still behind the ficus tree.

"Isn't this coming weekend Fast Sunday?" Nellie asked in an absent-minded manner. "I think we should all fast to ensure that Heavenly Father keeps looking out for us."

"I'm not fasting," said Quinn.

Nellie barely bothered to look in her direction. "It's my food," she said.

"Have a heart, honey," said Gavin.

Nellie looked about at the others, either assessing or judging, Gavin couldn't tell which. "I wonder if we should be ready to burn the house down if we're attacked," she mused. "The way the saints were prepared to burn Salt Lake City to the ground if the Army came in."

"Maybe we ought to be like the Indians in New England," said Quinn, "who gave food to the settlers, even though the settlers were stealing their land."

"Someone's trying to be PC again," Nellie muttered.

Gavin wondered how society had survived this long, if five people from the same town, with the same religious upbringing, couldn't hold a peaceful conversation without slashing away at each other. What chance did they have of getting along with people in Russia, or Pakistan, or New York?

They were simply going to have to do better. Gavin remembered watching late night movies as a boy, films like *Lifeboat* or *Mighty Joe Young* or *The Valley of Gwangi*. It constantly irritated him that there was always a jerk among the characters. Here was a story about shipwreck survivors trying to stay alive in a tiny boat on the wild sea. Did the audience really need an adversary in the cast? Wasn't just surviving the elements enough of an obstacle? But the directors always put those infuriating characters in the film. It used to drive Gavin nuts.

But perhaps it wasn't just a movie gimmick. Maybe those directors were on to something. There really *was* always a jerk in every group. Sometimes more than one.

Gavin thought back to every bishopric or stake presidency or high council he'd ever known. There had never been a time when he liked *everyone* in the group. Of course, he'd always felt that was his own failing.

But maybe it was just the nature of the beast.

"What if we simply blew a horn and invited anyone still in the neighborhood over for dinner?" asked Gavin. Everyone turned to look at him. "Wouldn't it be better to share what we had, and all live a few days longer, than…" He stopped when he saw the expression on everyone's faces. Even Quinn was sending daggers in his direction, clutching her baby fiercely. Maybe *he* was the jerk in the cast, he thought.

Fortunately, Jon seemed to sense the need for action and took over the conversation. "If it's the Last Days," he said, "there's still one prophecy that hasn't come to pass yet. At least that we know of. Maybe it's taking place right now and going something like this." Everyone seemed to relax a little, now that they could return to pretense. Jon started his story, and everyone listened in relief.

The Ten Tribes Return

Reed slowly stepped out of the car and plodded toward the door at the back of the garage leading to the kitchen. It had been another long day at work, and as the bishop of his local ward in Orem, he'd have to grab a quick dinner with Angela and the kids and then head off to do some counseling at the meetinghouse.

"Did you hear?" Angela asked as he came through the door.

"What?" he asked. He tried to give his wife a kiss, but she was too agitated.

"Don't you pay attention to what's happening in the world while you're at work?" she demanded. "Don't you even check Yahoo News once in a while?"

Reed was so pressed with duties at the office that he didn't take either of his two fifteen-minute breaks during the day, and he worked straight through lunch. Even so, the manager of the department had reduced everyone's pay by $200 a month. "What happened?" he asked. Short of hearing a temple was being rebuilt in Jerusalem, or the Prophet had asked everyone to relocate to Jackson County, Missouri, he wasn't sure he really cared.

"SETI has found extraterrestrial life!" Angela looked both scared and excited.

"What?" Reed reconsidered. If this was true, it might in fact be worthy of attention. But looking at his wife, he wondered if she'd just been watching the trailer for a new movie without realizing it.

"I didn't understand all of it," Angela went on breathlessly, "but apparently, they detected radio waves, and gamma rays, and some kind of electromagnetic radiation. They explained it all on the news, but I didn't understand much. Every station's been reporting it."

Reed remembered that his wife had dropped out of college and never finished her Biology degree when they were married thirteen years before. She loved news about science, but sometimes she blew it out of proportion. Like when she pointed out there'd been a minor earthquake in the same state where fracking was going on.

Some scientist at NASA had probably noticed another supernova or something. Something simple. He looked at his watch. He'd had to work more than an hour off the clock at the end of his workday to catch up with the heavy workload. His manager forbid employees to do it, but she also forbid them to rack up overtime. What else could you expect from a Gentile in Utah? "Is dinner ready?" he asked. "I've got to get to church."

"Oh, Reed," Angela said. "Don't you understand what this means?"

Reed moved to the table and sat down, hoping to prime the pump. The table wasn't even set yet. "So there was a radio signal," he said. "So what? It's not as if it means anything at all. They didn't actually get a message from anyone, did they?"

Angela sat down at the table across from him and reached over to hold his hand. "Reed, the scientists at SETI said they received all these signals months ago and have been working on them ever since." She paused, that frightened yet excited look still in her eyes. "They said they were forced to announce their findings because they expect contact any day now."

Reed closed his eyes. "Can't we talk about it over dinner, honey? I'm so hungry. It's been such a long day."

Angela gave him a long look he couldn't quite decipher and then stood up and went to the pantry. She opened a can of kidney beans, dumped them in a bowl, and poured a little Chinese sweet chili sauce over them. She stuck the bowl in the microwave and slammed the door. A minute later, she took them out, stirred them with a fork, and put the bowl in front of Reed. He frowned but began eating.

"Shouldn't you call the stake president?" she asked. "Or Salt Lake?"

Reed finished swallowing a large forkful of beans. "Why would I do that?"

Angela looked exasperated. She'd always maintained that as the person with the higher IQ, she should have gone on to have a career and let Reed stay home with their two kids. Reed sometimes grew tired of her superiority, but right now, he was in too much of a hurry to make an issue of it.

"Surely, it's the lost ten tribes coming back, don't you think?"

Reed stopped chewing. He wondered if his wife had completely lost her senses. She'd complained so much about how suffocating it was to stay at home. Maybe she'd finally flipped. He looked about. "Where are the kids?" he asked.

Angela waved away the question. "I gave Bradley and Samantha hot dogs an hour ago. They're in the living room watching *Close Encounters of the Third Kind.*"

"Angela…"

"Don't you remember?" Angela persisted. "Back when we were in Institute?" She looked into Reed's eyes, and Reed could only wonder what she saw. He wasn't sure what he saw in hers, either.

"We studied a lot of things," he said carefully. He paused and then added, "Can I get something to drink?"

Angela closed her eyes and then stood up and pulled a can of orange soda from the fridge, slapping it down on the table in front of Reed. He decided he'd better use his bishopric skills and de-escalate the situation. "Honey, tell me what's bothering you."

"Don't you remember Brigham Young saying there was life on the sun?"

Reed popped open the soda and took a sip. Angela hadn't even given him a glass. "He was just speaking as a man, not as a prophet," he pointed out.

"And one of Joseph Smith's friends claimed that Joseph said there were men on the moon, the ones dressed like Quakers?" She frowned, and Reed hoped she realized how irrational she was being.

"We don't know Joseph Smith really said that, honey."

Angela began pacing back and forth across the kitchen. "Remember when I showed you my great-great-grandfather's Patriarchal Blessing? The one that said he would preach to the inhabitants of the moon and other planets?"

Reed was going to have to refer her to an LDS psychiatrist. She was going off the deep end. Perhaps he should have allowed her to work part-time while the kids were at school, as she'd asked time after time. It definitely would've helped with the household budget. Of course, it wasn't as if the children were screaming toddlers. Bradley was eleven and Samantha twelve. Angela certainly wasn't being reduced to speaking baby talk every day. What was so hard about staying home and vacuuming once in a while? Perhaps he should have agreed to Angela's suggestion and let his wife be the breadwinner.

Of course, then he never would have been called to serve as bishop. And he still had hopes of moving further up the ladder.

"Yes," said Reed, "and my grandmother's blessing said she'd live to see the Second Coming. And we both know she died two years ago." He looked at his beans and wasn't sure he should take another bite. He'd watched her prepare them, but he couldn't help but worry she might have added something he shouldn't be eating. "Some stake patriarchs aren't as inspired as others," he went on. "They're not *the* Prophet."

"Hey, Mom," Samantha said, sticking her head in the kitchen, "it's the woman from *A Christmas Story*."

"Yes, dear," said Angela. "She's quite a good actress, isn't she? Go back and finish watching the movie." Samantha left, and Angela turned back to Reed. He decided he'd take another bite, after all. Angela watched him a moment and then continued. "Brigham Young said that Joseph Smith told him the ten tribes were on a portion of land separated from the Earth, and that the portion would be let down one day in the polar regions, that when the ice melts the tribes will come down from the north."

She looked at him triumphantly. "Global warming is part of Heavenly Father's plan. The ten tribes are coming back. Any day now." She looked at Reed. "Aren't you excited? Don't you care?" She looked as if she were about to knock his bowl of beans onto the floor, so Reed quickly took another bite.

As Reed chewed, he thought about what he should say. In all likelihood, the SETI scientists were either wrong or blatantly lying, trying to drum up a little interest in their decades-long research failure. You could never really trust anything a scientist said. It was just as well his wife hadn't become one. And aliens were merely the stuff of science fiction.

Obviously, with all the gods out there, there were plenty of other inhabited planets, but that didn't mean any of the people on them would ever be able to communicate with the inhabitants on any other. There was a reason nothing traveled faster than the speed of light, a reason there could never be any communication between different civilizations. To discover other humans on other planets, also in the image of God, would be giving people proof of God's existence, and God forced his followers to work on faith, not proof. There were no Vulcans or Betazoids out there. And definitely no Wookiees.

Reed looked at Angela, who'd stopped pacing and was staring at him imploringly. He thought for a long moment and then nodded. "Honey," he said soothingly, "why don't you come with me to my office, and we'll call the stake president together?" He forced a smile, hoping it was convincing.

Angela collapsed into a chair. "Thank you, Reed. Thank you." She grasped his hand again.

They stood up and walked through the living room toward the back of the house to Reed's office. Reed turned to Angela. "Why aren't you having the kids watch the news?" he asked. "They must still be reporting on it." If the woman wasn't completely delusional to begin with. He still wasn't sure that the movie trailer simply hadn't been playing on two different stations.

"The news is too scary," she replied. "They're making it sound dangerous to have aliens visit." She shook her head. "And the Church hasn't really produced any good DVDs about the ten tribes coming back. So Spielberg was the best I could do."

Reed sat at his desk and motioned for Angela to sit in the overstuffed easy chair a few feet away. He called the stake president, asked a few questions, and then put down the phone. He stared at his wife.

"Well?" she demanded.

"He's already called Salt Lake when he heard the news," Reed said slowly. "The First Presidency isn't making any public statements yet." He frowned and looked at his planner on the desk in front of him. The stake president had seemed unnaturally worried. But none of this made any sense at all. Why wouldn't the Church jump at the chance to show everyone they knew what was really going on? Why didn't the Prophet at least call the U.S. president and tell him how to react, what to expect, what to do? Wasn't that the whole reason for having a prophet, to lead people in times like this?

Reed glanced at his watch, still frowning. For that matter, why hadn't the Prophet alerted the President about 9-1-1 before it happened? Or warned the Haitians about that massive earthquake about to kill two hundred thousand people? Why did he encourage Church members to donate so much money to Proposition 8, when same sex marriage was inevitable to begin with?

What good was having a Prophet, if the best he could tell you was "Read your scriptures and pay your tithing?"

Reed picked up the planner and flipped through it absentmindedly. Perhaps it was another part of not wanting to give people evidence, to force them to continue living by faith, even in the midst of miracles such as this. The ten tribes, he thought in amazement. Angela was right. He never thought he'd live to see the day.

He looked up at his wife and forced another smile. "Can you come with me to the church tonight?" he asked. "I want you there in case we hear anything from Salt Lake." The Prophet just *had* to say something this time.

Angela smiled and nodded happily. "The kids'll be okay on their own. They've got *ET* to watch when they finish *Close Encounters*." She giggled in relief, putting her hand over her mouth. "I told them they could stay up till 10:00 tonight. It's a night we'll always remember." She stood up and twirled around the room. "Reed, it's the Last Days! The ten tribes are coming back! Jesus will be here soon!" She hugged herself and then ran over and kissed Reed on the lips.

Reed wasn't completely sure this still wasn't some kind of PR stunt dreamt up by SETI, which might explain why Salt Lake was so quiet on the subject, but he and Angela would listen to the radio on the way to the chapel, and Reed might try to stay up late and watch CNN when they got back home. If all this were true, he might even just miss work in the morning. He smiled when he thought about what his manager would say to that.

Reed took Angela's hand and they walked back through the living room together, said good-bye to the children, and headed out the kitchen back to the garage. They were just pulling out of the driveway when the first explosions from the alien invasion began.

The Gathering 10

"Mormons also had dances to keep up their spirits in pioneer days," said Quinn when Jon was through. The baby was back asleep on the floor.

"You didn't like my story?" he asked, looking a bit miffed.

"I'm just saying."

"And who would *you* dance with anyway?" asked Nellie, not looking up from her runner.

"Aren't you about finished with that damn thing?" Quinn asked in return.

Nellie was silent a moment as she carefully tied a knot. "A true work of art takes both time and patience." She set the fabric down and took a sip of water. "Just like crafting a pure and obedient soul."

"Oh, brother."

Gavin closed his eyes. The bickering never seemed to stop. It was as if the only way they could keep the peace was by stuffing their mouths with the nonsense words of fabulous stories like a gag. Only he wasn't sure those words weren't suffocating them instead.

But he did want to live. And people would do whatever it took to survive. They'd eat their dead companions after crashing their plane in the Andes. They'd eat them while stranded in a snowy pass on their way to California. Perhaps what they were doing now wasn't so terribly different.

Was that also the reason for all the General Conference talks twice a year, year after year after year? Gavin had always wondered why Mormon "revivals" were so dull, when they were supposed to be regenerating everyone's commitment to the gospel. If Gavin and his housemates needed to tell fanciful stories to get through their present ordeal, maybe Church leaders were doing the same thing. Earth life even under the best of circumstances was always described by the prophets as something that had to be "endured," perhaps just as much a matter of starving or rationing as their current predicament.

Were the leaders right now plotting to eat the Indian guides leading them through the Sierras? Or the pilot who had descended too soon before fully crossing the Andes? It suddenly struck Gavin that demanding he give up the life he wanted to live was a way of serving him up as dinner for everyone else. Was this the only way Mormon leaders could offer genuine sustenance to their followers?

Gavin felt as if he'd finally understood what letters were, after seeing the alphabet in front of him for years. Understanding the talks of the apostles as a form of cannibalism somehow seemed to make everything else fall into place.

"Is it snack time yet?" asked Emma. "I don't need much, just a bite of something."

"I can help you in the kitchen," Jon offered.

Nellie looked bored but nodded. She led them down the hallway, and a few moments later, they came back carrying little boxes of Sun-Maid raisins. Everyone took the opportunity to chew in silence, but Gavin was contemplating what he would say next. It was his turn to tell a story. He thought about all the times in his life when he'd just shut up. If he was going to die soon, he wanted to do it as a brave man. He'd always believed that staying away from men showed how strong and courageous he was, but maybe that belief had instead been his greatest weakness.

Or maybe not.

Would he *never* know how to live his life before it was over?

Was everyone else in this house thinking the same thing?

Nellie threaded her needle with green thread.

Gavin was starving, he thought. He was absolutely starving. He put his empty raisin box on the coffee table, took a sip of water from his purple cup, and decided to tell the story he needed to tell.

The Kind Heart of a (Near) Perfect God

"As man is, God once was. As God is, man may become." Alvin had heard those words many times throughout his life, and now that he was meeting Heavenly Father for the first time since dying, he was anxious to know if it was true. He must have known all about Him back in the Pre-Existence, but he couldn't remember the specifics. He did remember all the friends he'd known then. He was happy to see many of them again. But the details of Heavenly Father's life—no, he just didn't remember. Had that been kept secret back in the Pre-Earth life until after the test of mortal existence?

Sacred, not secret.

He sat down in front of the golden throne and looked hesitantly at his Father in Heaven. Afraid to lock eyes, Alvin looked around the room. There were chandeliers hanging from the high ceiling with hundreds, perhaps thousands, of glittering crystals. Marble columns were scattered about the room with ornate vases of unrecognizable colored stone set on top, with exotic flowers flowing over the lip of each. There was a fragrance in the room Alvin couldn't quite identify, but whatever it was, it was lovely. And then there was God sitting majestically on His throne, on green velvet cushions. He looked old, maybe in his sixties, but young, too, perhaps twenty-five, a man in his prime. How odd that He could create two completely different impressions at the same time.

"Welcome, my son," said Elohim.

"It's so good to see You again after all this time," Alvin replied.

"It's only been a few moments since you were here before."

Alvin nodded.

"I sense you have some questions for me?" Elohim rubbed his beard thoughtfully. It looked both richly brown and starkly white at the same time. "New arrivals always do." He shook his head. "You'd think you hadn't already spent millions of years with me."

Had he, Alvin wondered? He remembered lots of classes, lots of playing with friends, lots of imagining their glorious mortal existence to come, but not much time with their Father Himself. And then, of course, while on Earth, he only remembered spending his Sundays talking about Joseph Smith, not Heavenly Father, and not even much about Jesus.

And never about Heavenly Mother. Whoever she was.

"All my life," Alvin began, "I always felt closer to You than to Jesus." He glanced toward the door to make sure Jesus was still outside and couldn't hear. He'd hardly felt close to either, to be honest. But he'd fantasized about Heavenly Father's mortal life during most of his own.

Had He ever failed a Physics test? Had He been a goldsmith? A pizza maker? Did He have zits? Dandruff? He'd been a normal, average person just like Alvin. Only average people didn't become gods, did they, so maybe He'd been the quarterback even when alive. "Jesus was perfect, but

You…You had been a mere mortal before. Sinful like the rest of us. And You persevered and made it to Your own Celestial Kingdom." It was an example he knew almost nothing about, but which had driven him for decades.

Had Heavenly Father ever wet the bed when He was a boy? Had He ever stolen a candy bar and then brought it back to the store with an apology note? Perhaps He'd looked in His father's bedside drawer and found His father's condoms. And porn.

Had Heavenly Father even once looked at porn when He was a human? Could someone who had ever done such a thing become a god?

Elohim looked at Alvin with a bemused expression.

"I just wanted to know…I wanted to know…" *Everything*, though Alvin. It was this specific man's life he had needed to know everything about if he were ever to have a chance to emulate Him and survive Earth life.

Why hadn't Church leaders given members anything at all to go on? It was like trying to learn to be a prima ballerina without ever watching a single ballet. "I just wanted to know…" He just couldn't say it. "I…I wanted to know…"

"If I liked sucking dick back when I was alive," Elohim finished. "I know. I've known your thoughts all along."

Alvin was both mortified and relieved. "Well?" he asked. "Can you *really* understand me? *Really and truly*? Do you *really* know what I've been through trying to be celibate all these years in the Church?" He had felt so terribly alone for so horribly long.

Elohim stood up and motioned for Alvin to approach. Alvin did so cautiously, but when he was within a few feet of the great god, Elohim pulled him close in a tremendous bear hug. "Of course I do, my son."

Alvin was hugging God. *God.* He had never felt so loved in his entire existence. Finally. After waiting such a painfully long time. It was a feeling he'd craved for longer than he could remember. For even longer than he'd been alive on Earth. He relaxed and luxuriated in the feel of complete, total bliss. He wished he could record the feeling and play it back on an endless loop. Then he abruptly noticed something else terrible and pulled back.

"What is it, my son?"

"You know perfectly well what it is."

Elohim shrugged. "So you're getting an erection. True love is sexual love, too. It's perfectly all right." He grinned. "And when I use the word 'perfect,' you know I mean it."

Alvin frowned. "I don't understand. Are You gay, too?" It was the question he'd wanted answered for years and years and years, feeling it was a terrible sin even to formulate the question in the first place.

"Oh, I struggled with same-sex attraction when I was a human back on my planet billions of years ago." He looked at Alvin and chuckled. "I don't know why you should be so shocked. If you didn't believe a gay man was still capable of becoming a god, why did you stay celibate all those years?"

"I...I..."

He nodded. "I know. So many Mormons are quite narrow-minded." He sat back down and motioned for Alvin to sit on the floor at his feet, on a tiny throw rug that seemed to be spun of pure gold. "It doesn't mean I am."

Alvin stared at Elohim on his cushioned throne, majestic paintings of galaxies and nebulae hanging on the walls on either side of him. This man had gone through the same trials he'd gone through. Why in the name of all that was holy hadn't the Church taught them more about the mortal weaknesses of Elohim than about the perfection of Jesus, who was so far removed from their experience that no human could ever truly relate to him?

"So when do I become straight?" asked Alvin. "Can I get married to a woman now? You must have hundreds of wives. Thousands, to have so many billions of spirit children. How did you finally become straight?" He'd thought it would happen automatically the moment he died, kind of like a spiritual resurrection. Some miraculous change in the twinkling of an eye.

Elohim laughed. "Son, this is who you *are*. It's not going to change."

Alvin's mouth opened in horror. Elohim reached down and patted him on the head. "It's not as bad as all that," He said soothingly. "There was a Savior on the world where I grew up, too. His Atonement is still in effect. It was an eternal Atonement."

Now Alvin frowned again. "I don't understand."

Elohim sighed and then nodded. "Okay. Let me show you." He closed His eyes for a moment as if concentrating very hard, and a few seconds later, the door opened. A handsome angel, also about twenty-five, walked up to the throne. Alvin scrambled out of the way. Elohim lifted His robe and let His ten-inch erection stab out into the room. The angel kneeled down and took the tremendous organ into his mouth. Five minutes later, the angel stood up and left the room.

"What the hell was that?" Alvin demanded. He was trembling, but he felt his own member straining against his garments.

Elohim laughed, a hearty sound. "The ministering angels don't officially get to have eternal sex like those who make it to the top degree of the Celestial Kingdom. But I just don't have it in me to deprive them completely. So I let them suck me off." He shrugged. "Sometimes, I suck them off. And then my Savior's Atonement kicks in, and I'm forgiven and am perfect again and keep ruling my universe."

Alvin's mouth fell open.

"You sure are cute when you do that."

Alvin closed his mouth. "I don't understand," he repeated.

"Oh, dear, this discussion is becoming rather tedious," Elohim said wearily. "It's like this—even two thousand women will just never really do it for me. And since I'm a god, I get to make some of the rules." He waved away Alvin's question. "Yes, some laws are eternal, and heterosexuality is one of them. But you were a boss down on Earth, a company owner. You know perfectly well that bosses don't follow the same rules as employees."

"But…but…"

"And I'm using the word 'perfectly' on purpose."

"Father," Alvin said softly, almost unable to speak, "are You trying to tell me…I'm finally free?"

Elohim smiled, the sweetest expression Alvin had ever seen. "I love you, my son. I love you."

"Really and truly?" Alvin shook his head. "All these years, I felt You were disgusted by my very existence."

"I can only say it so many times," said Elohim. "Look, there's only one way to fully convince you. Come here." He pointed to a spot directly in front of Him. Alvin approached cautiously. "Turn around." Alvin did so, unsure what was going on. Then he felt Heavenly Father's hands on his back, lifting his robe. He felt his cheeks being spread, and then a moment later…

It was the most beautiful moment of his life. God loved him. In the fullest sense of the word. And with ten inches inside him, Alvin felt full.

Elohim took his time, made sure Alvin enjoyed his first sexual experience, and then He pulled out, dropped Alvin's robe back down, and His own as well.

"Are we good then?" asked Elohim. "You okay?"

"Yes, Father."

Elohim smiled. Such a warm man. "Now go on and pick out a dozen or so wives from the Wife Pool," He said. "And a good twenty or so male angels from the Ministering Pool.

You can come back every thousand years or so and get a few more. So be on your way."

Alvin nodded. He took a chance and ran up to Elohim and kissed Him on the mouth before heading toward the door. When he opened it, he saw Jesus standing in the hallway, waiting to let the next person in. Jesus, that perfect man without a blemish on his soul, a man Alvin would never, never understand. But as it was this man's Atonement that would allow him to have the eternity he wanted, he had to be grateful at least for that. Jesus stared at him blankly, surely knowing what had just transpired. He looked as if he wanted to check his watch. Alvin dipped his head politely in respect and hurried off down the hallway to the Wife Pool.

He wondered if he could find one with hairy arms.

The Gathering 11

When Gavin finished speaking, he looked at the others in the room with their mouths hanging open.

"You know what Heavenly Father would say if *he* saw you looking so inviting," said Gavin.

"I—I don't know what to say," said Nellie. "You've always been a trial to me. Always. And now you're deliberately inviting God to smite us."

"I'm no gayer now than I ever was," Gavin replied. "Still a virgin when it comes to men."

"Yes, but…but now you're *talking* about it."

"I loved the way you depicted women as accessories," said Quinn with a smile. "That was a very Mormon story."

"The Church doesn't treat us as accessories!" Emma protested. As if on cue, Jon pointed to his red plastic glass on the coffee table, and Emma handed it to him. Gavin kept his face blank. "If anything, the Church puts us on a pedestal."

"Well, we're all equal in the face of death," said Jon. "No one's special here." He took a sip of water. It looked like blood.

Nellie smiled craftily. "Aren't we?" she asked. "Is it just coincidence that more women in this room have survived the Apocalypse than men?"

"Yes," Jon replied quickly. "It *is* coincidence."

"Four to two?" said Nellie. "Statistically improbable."

"What do you know about statistics, Sister Askew?" asked Quinn.

"Enough," she replied with that same crafty smile. Then she stopped smiling and looked at both Gavin and Jon. "And if someone does break in, I can just bet who the Lord will let them take first."

There was silence for a long moment, broken finally by Quinn singing, "There is beauty all around…" Nellie glared at her and she stopped.

There was more silence, until Gavin worked up the nerve to say what had been on his mind ever since Jon had taken refuge in the house. "I wish I'd had sex with a man at least once in my life."

All heads swiveled in his direction.

"You'd be dead right now if you had," said Nellie.

Gavin shrugged. "Maybe that wouldn't be such a high price to pay," he replied. "I mean, what if there's nothing on the Other Side? What if there *is* no Other Side?" Nellie worked on a flower, ignoring him. "Even if there is eternal life, what if I'm gay forever, and have to be celibate for eternity?"

"It won't be like that, Gavin," Emma said soothingly.

"Every time I eat a piece of cheesecake," Gavin went on, "or hear a pretty song on the radio, or see a beautiful flower, I concentrate completely on that moment of ecstasy. I imagine eternity to be a place where I have CDs and DVDs of all my most exquisite moments in life, and I can replay them over and over, always experiencing the joy I felt the moment I experienced it in life."

"That's beautiful," said Emma.

"And if that's all I have, if I'm never going to be worthy of anything better in the afterlife, I want at least one beautiful moment with another man, to play over and over and over."

"If it's with a man," said Nellie, still not looking up, "it won't be beautiful."

"Well, don't look at me," said Jon, holding up his hands as if stopping a runaway shopping cart. "I'm not gay."

Gavin shrugged. "And I'm not straight. But I've had an awful lot of straight sex."

"Not so much," said Nellie.

Gavin looked at her. Had she always been this mean? Surely, he didn't want to spend an eternity with this woman.

"I don't want to have sex with you," said Jon.

Gavin nodded.

"Sex, sex, sex," Nellie said. "Everyone keeps talking about sex. Is that the only thing you people think about? I thought I already told you to cut it out."

"Isn't sex the whole purpose behind getting to the Celestial Kingdom?" asked Quinn. "How can we *not* think about it? No one wants to be a ministering angel, even if they're in the Celestial Kingdom. They want the top spot, because it's only in the top spot you can have sex for eternity."

"We want the top spot because it's only there we can become gods," said Nellie.

Quinn laughed. "And being a god means having sex billions of times so we can populate planet after planet. It's on the mind of every man I've ever dated."

"That's beside the point."

"That's the *whole* point."

"It isn't."

"Oh, my god," said Jon, "this bickering is even worse than listening to these god-awful stories."

Nellie gave him a withering look for taking the Lord's name in vain. "My house, my rules," she said.

Jon nodded.

"Anyway," said Nellie, "*I* have a much better story that everyone will like." She looked at Gavin. He looked instead at Jon, his face still blank, and took a sip of water as she began.

Dawn of the Dead

The alarm rang at 6:30, as it did every morning, and I groggily reached over to slap the off button. I sat up and swung my legs to the floor, stretching lazily. Elder Murdoch still had his covers tucked under his chin, pretending he didn't hear the alarm. He always had a harder time waking up than I did, and as he'd been feeling poorly lately, I decided to let him sleep in. I staggered to the kitchen of our tiny apartment in downtown Cleveland, feeling like a zombie.

I felt like a zombie most of the time lately, to be honest. In a few hours, Elder Murdoch and I had a teaching appointment scheduled with a young couple. It was Saturday and they'd both be home from work. But while I should be rejoicing at the golden opportunity, instead I felt lifeless, moving about as if I was still alive but really dead inside.

It had all started a few weeks ago when my companion and I were doing some street contacting. "Oh, my heck," I said, pointing. "Look at that man's T-shirt."

Elder Murdoch looked. A white man about forty-five was wearing a shirt with some offensive words on it. A woman who didn't appear to be his wife was berating him. "What do we want?" the T-shirt proclaimed. "A cure for Tourette's. When do we want it? Cunt."

"Don't look at stuff like that, Elder Lawrence," my companion chided. "You'll lose the Spirit."

And it had happened. I'd been out on my mission for nine months, and I'd just been transferred to this district to serve under Elder Murdoch. I was hoping this would be my last stint as junior companion. But to make sure that was the case, I had to really shine and show the mission president I possessed what it took to be a senior. Only I kept thinking of that T-shirt, and other curse words kept flooding my brain. Cock. Tits. Pussy. Ass. Fuck. Fuck. Fuck.

We weren't allowed to talk to women, but that only seemed to make things worse. We'd stop a man on the street to discuss the importance of families, and instead of reflecting on the beauty of Christ's atonement, I'd be thinking, "I want to see you fuck your girlfriend." We'd knock on someone's door and ask the woman who answered if her husband was at home, and I'd think, "Is he licking you every night? Are you sucking his dick?"

Was there such a thing as spiritual Tourette's?

Maybe my decline had started even earlier than I realized, and I just hadn't noticed, the way a person could have a contagious cold hours before he showed the first symptoms.

I never said a word about my struggle. Elder Murdoch had enough on his mind as it was. He'd developed a toothache, suffered with that for several days, then ended up needing dental surgery, and had suffered for several days after that. He'd been calling the mission president the last few days, asking for permission to see a doctor, but President Cantwell said we'd wasted enough time not proselytizing. He told Elder

Murdoch to take some aspirin and man up. We didn't even have the zone leaders come to give my companion a blessing.

We'd come home at 8:00 last night, Elder Murdoch saying he felt "lousy." He went straight to bed, and I was left struggling to read the latest issue of the *Ensign*. There was an article about Joseph Smith's seer stone and how he used it to translate the Book of Mormon. It was mildly disturbing because I'd always thought he'd translated the actual plates themselves, but now the Church was saying that he'd instead had a little brown rock which he put in a hat. Then he buried his face in the hat and read off the letters one at a time as the Spirit directed him.

In my perverse mood, I couldn't help remembering a scene from one of my favorite childhood movies, *A Christmas Story*, which my family watched religiously every year. "Be sure to drink your Ovaltine," I imagined Joseph writing out, one letter at a time.

Why did these awful thoughts keep bursting forth from my head against my will?

It didn't help that my cousin Andrew was emailing me weekly, trying to "open my eyes." He'd been censored from my official missionary account, but I still emailed a few people on my own personal email. Another one of my failings. Andrew kept pointing out things he felt were proof positive the Church wasn't true, but mostly, the issues he raised simply didn't matter to me.

"You guys let your brains rot," he said in frustration last Preparation Day. "It's as if you all deliberately infect yourselves with Mad Cow disease."

"I memorize one new scripture verse a week," I'd written in reply. But even as I wrote it, I could imagine his response. "You're a regular intellectual giant."

"Fuck!" I whispered at my desk after finishing the article, not wanting to wake Elder Murdoch. I closed the magazine. "Shit!" Why was I losing my testimony? I was soulless without it, truly the undead. I'd knelt beside my bed last night and prayed for forty minutes, but it seemed I wasn't worthy to receive an answer.

Now it was Saturday, and I somehow had to kindle a spark of Spirit within myself before our teaching appointment at 10:00. I ate a bowl of Sugar Smacks and then went to the bathroom to shower. Knowing my companion was not likely to intrude, I allowed myself to lather up and stroke myself a few moments. I was so tempted to complete what I'd started, but I had to be good. I twisted the dial until the water turned cold and finished rinsing off.

I put on my white garments, fingering the embroidered symbols, but also fingering my penis through the fabric. Then I pulled on my suit pants, zipped up, and cinched my belt tightly. I'd leave the white shirt and tie off till we were ready to leave the apartment. Elder Murdoch was still sound asleep. Lucky bastard. I longed to be unconscious like that, without thoughts, if only for a few hours.

I remembered a scene from the original *Dawn of the Dead*, a movie I'd been forbidden to see because of its rating. A zombie nun's habit was caught in the door the hero was trying to close. If he couldn't close it, all the zombies would get in and kill the survivors. But the nun, even as a zombie, had enough sweetness left to pull her habit out of the way and let the hero close the door.

I was still haunted by the many images I'd seen in R-rated films, the filthy words I'd heard, and the base thoughts that had been generated. And I was haunted continually by all the other sins I'd committed over the years as well. Sin was like a virus that spread throughout a community. But I was a missionary now, spreading righteousness. I could atone for my mistakes.

I wondered what it was like for Mormons who died in their apostasy and went to Outer Darkness. Perhaps they were chased about forever by the damned spirits who'd been cast out with Satan and never had bodies of their own, always clawing away at the resurrected sinners and trying to get inside them.

I thought of the checkout girl at Safeway two days ago I wanted to get inside.

Fuck! Stop thinking that shit!

I remembered my father clapping his hand on my shoulder at the airport, saying, "I'd rather have my son come back from his mission in a coffin than come back having lost his virtue."

"Or his testimony," my mother had added, wiping away a tear.

I forced myself to read a few sections from the Doctrine and Covenants. Then I had my morning prayer. Elder Murdoch was still asleep. I looked at my watch. It was after 9:00. I went over to nudge him.

"Wake up, sleepyhead," I said. "We have to get to our appointment." I shook his shoulder again. He didn't even murmur in protest.

I frowned. "Elder Murdoch," I said more forcefully. "Wake up. You've slept long enough." I shook him harder.

Oh, my heck. He wasn't moving. I shook harder and called his name again. Then I put my hand against his face. It was cold.

I stepped quickly away from the bed, my arms crossed tightly over my chest. "Fuck!" I said aloud. "Fuck, fuck, fuck!"

Then I glanced about nervously, expecting God to strike me down, too. Elder Murdoch had told me last night that he thought the mission president was wrong, that if he still felt lousy today we would go to an Urgent Care center after our appointment. I sat on my bed and looked over at him. What in the world could have happened? Perhaps he'd developed blood poisoning or something. He was in perfect shape except for that tooth problem.

I should call the zone leaders. I should call the mission president.

I looked at my watch. I would just have time to make that appointment if I left now. Was this a trial to see if I would keep doing missionary work even when I had an excuse not to? Maybe I should go teach the young couple by myself, prove to the president I was ready to be a senior by taking on the responsibility all alone. Perhaps this was Satan trying to stop the lesson, the one day the couple would be in tune with the Spirit and convert.

Of course, it was against mission rules to go anywhere without one's companion. But there wasn't enough time to call another companionship and ask someone else to come along. Or even to call one of the local ward members and ask him to fill in for a few hours. What was the bigger sin, leaving my companion or not baptizing?

I sat on my bed and looked at Elder Murdoch. I had to make a decision quickly. But I felt that spiritual Tourette's building up again. I remembered Elder Murdoch had told me once he wasn't circumcised. I'd never seen an uncircumcised penis before, never allowing myself to look at my companion in the front when he stepped out of the shower, though I'd stolen a glance at his ass a time or two. Would it be terrible to take a peek at his dick now? Elder Murdoch wasn't here to mind the invasion.

I pulled the covers down and looked at the bottom half of my companion's garments. I could see dark pubic hair underneath the fabric. I took a deep breath and pulled down the garments. I gently reached down and touched his penis, pulling the foreskin back and forth over the head of his dick.

Then it was as if I could see the entire scene from outside myself.

I was a depraved pervert. I was even getting a hard-on. And I was straight.

Though maybe I didn't entirely hate the thought of penises, I realized.

Fuck.

I pulled Elder Murdoch's garments back up and dragged his blanket up over his chest. I needed to go teach that young couple and bring them to the Church. They'd be my first baptisms in eight months. I was here to spread the gospel.

I thought about my cousin Andrew, gritting my teeth. He was a host, a carrier, infecting me with doubt. Once an apostate's teeth were in you, the outcome of the virus was clear, even if you didn't die immediately. You eventually started biting chunks out of someone's neck, spreading the infection further. But I would stay true. Or die trying. I reached down and fingered Elder Murdoch's penis again.

It was a sin to leave my companion.

So perhaps I shouldn't leave him.

I went to the kitchen and pulled our sharpest knife out of the drawer, and then I returned to the bedroom. I slid into bed next to my companion and looked at the blade. I didn't pray. Elder Murdoch's eyes were closed, but he wasn't praying, either. I took a deep breath. I had to stop this sickness before it went any further. The first slice was deep, and I felt a stirring in my groin.

"Fuck! Shit!"

The second slice was even deeper, but this time I smiled.

I wondered if I would eat spirit brains in hell, or if someone else would be eating mine. I closed my eyes and calmly waited to find out the answer.

The Gathering 12

"What a beautiful story, Nellie," said Gavin gently. The others looked at him in confusion. "I always knew the only good gay was a dead gay," he added in a less agreeable tone.

Nellie shrugged. "I tell it like I see it."

"You always have."

"Isn't that what you like about me?"

Gavin didn't respond.

"I have to say I was a bit shocked to hear you using some of those words," Jon said, looking uncomfortable.

Nellie smiled smugly. "I'm not as ignorant as you all seem to think." She touched her hair as if making sure it was in place. "I'm just righteous is all."

Jon and Emma locked eyes for a moment, and then Jon stole a glance at Gavin. He looked almost sorry enough that he might yet be willing to offer up his body to Gavin before this was all over.

"It's almost 1:00," said Quinn. "Can we take a break and eat something?"

Nellie stood. "How about creamed corn?" she asked. "We can use the last of the butter, and I'll add some pepper, too."

"Not too much pepper," said Emma, putting her hand on her chest.

"And not too much butter," said Gavin. "My cholesterol…" He stopped when he realized how foolish he sounded.

"I'll help you," said Emma. The two women headed to the kitchen.

"I have to hand it to you, Gavin," said Jon. "You're quite the saint." He seemed to be looking at Gavin's crotch. When he realized what he was doing, he quickly looked away.

"I'm never getting married," said Quinn. She was holding the baby's hand, but the baby was looking at something on the wall. Perhaps the framed photo of the St. George temple. Was the infant seeing a vision, Gavin wondered? Watching angels coming to welcome them to the Spirit World?

Gavin shook his head in disgust.

"Not even in the Millennium?" asked Jon. He was looking at Quinn's breasts now while her eyes were diverted.

"If I'm good enough to get into the Millennium without a man, I'm good enough to get into the Celestial Kingdom."

"I don't think it works like that," said Jon. He looked thoughtful for a moment. "Gavin holds the priesthood and could probably marry us in the next day or two. It won't be a temple marriage, but it'll put us on the road to a happy eternity."

"What will Emma say?" Quinn replied with a smile.

"She's already married. You and I aren't. Heavenly Father is giving us a chance to make things right. That's how trials work."

Quinn laughed. "You don't want to know what I think about how all this works," she replied. She leaned over and kissed the baby on the forehead. The baby giggled. For some reason, that seemed to make Quinn sad.

Nellie walked back into the living room and held up a hand. "The gas is out," she said simply. "We'll eat cold creamed corn with pepper. No use adding any butter if it's not hot." She turned around and headed back to the kitchen. She and Emma came back a few minutes later and handed bowls of cold corn to everyone. They ate in silence.

Gavin didn't know which was worse, the silence or the storytelling. He wished the end would come soon, one way or the other. He carried the empty bowls back to the kitchen. Quinn tried to wash them, but Gavin waved her away and washed them himself. Then he returned to the others in the living room.

Why hadn't they thought to save a two-year supply of crossword puzzles? Or Sudoku? They did have a few jigsaw puzzles, but working on them would require a degree of teamwork he suspected the group didn't have.

"Okay," said Jon, "whose turn is it?"

"I'll go next, if that's okay with everyone," Emma said, cuddling up against Jon, who put his hand on her leg. No one objected to Emma's offer. Gavin expected no one really cared at this point. Nellie picked up her embroidery, and Emma began.

The Flaming Sword in the Snow

Melanie pulled up to her parents' home in Spanish Fork and turned off the engine. Her sister Deidre and brother-in-law Thomas must already be there. Melanie could see their Ford Fiesta behind her parents' two twin Focuses in the driveway. Or was that Foci?

It was snowing pretty heavily this evening, and Melanie wasn't sure if she should have canceled her attendance at the weekly family dinner. Going home on Sundays, even for a few hours, was like trying to travel back in time and pretend she still believed in Santa Claus. But Deidre would be giving birth within a couple of months to her first child, and that would really change the dynamic of the visits, eliminating what little mature conversation there was now, so Melanie had pushed on and driven through the snow.

"Hi, Mom!" she said when her mother greeted her at the door, along with a sweltering wave of heat from the foyer. Melanie's mother kept the house at 80 degrees all winter. How her parents could afford the gas bill she didn't know. The two women hugged and then headed straight for the dining room. Thomas and Deidre and Melanie's father were already seated at the table. Melanie hadn't been *that* late. She glanced at her watch. Five minutes. Hardly the end of the world considering the snow.

Mom ushered Melanie to her seat, and then Dad blessed the food. As soon as everyone said amen, hands reached out immediately to grab the serving plates and bowls in front of them. "How have you been feeling, Deidre?" Melanie asked, noting the ever-growing stomach.

"Tired," she replied. "Sixty-six more days of this. I can hardly wait for B-Day."

"You'll get good at carrying before long," Thomas comforted her, patting her hand. "By the time we've had our fourth or fifth, you'll be an old pro."

"There's nothing more important than family," Mom said with a smile.

Deidre asked Mom to pass the carrots. Melanie asked about Thomas's work as a civil attorney, then about Mom's genealogy research and Dad's calling as Boy Scout leader. They all reported nominal advancements in their lives, a hard-to-find birth date of some great-great-great aunt, and a boy who'd advanced up from Tenderfoot. Melanie felt guilty that she didn't really care. It was just that every opportunity to have a human moment with them always seemed to turn into an advertisement for the Church. She could hardly wait until she got married and could start making excuses not to attend the family dinners. Of course, until she had her first baby, she'd still be expected to come. After that as well, but at least with a husband and a baby, she could get out of it.

Too bad she didn't want to get married. Or have a baby. Both of those commitments would entail a great deal of inconvenience *every* day, not just on Sundays.

"What's the latest from the Congo?" Melanie asked, dabbing some butter on a second piece of bread.

"Dan was just promoted to senior companion," Dad said proudly. "He'll be district leader before long."

"No, I meant how was the work coming along?" Melanie persisted.

Dad looked confused. "He was just made senior companion," he repeated, his brows furrowed.

Melanie then asked about her other brother, Hunter, away at BYU-Idaho studying business. "How are his classes going?" she asked.

"Oh, Hunter's dating a really nice girl up there," Mom replied. She looked at Melanie's father and grinned. "We may be hearing wedding bells again soon."

Melanie gave up and concentrated on the tuna casserole in front of her. She didn't eat meat, only fish, and after three successive visits in a row last year when she refused to eat the meal her mother had cooked, Mom finally began making vegetarian or fish dishes. That meant something. She could hardly ignore the fact that after twenty-five minutes around the table, no one else in the family had asked a single question about her. As an unmarried woman, she wasn't relevant.

But she did get the fish. Her existence was at least being acknowledged. It was more than some of her single Mormon girlfriends ever got.

After dinner, Melanie and Deidre helped Mom clear the table and wash the dishes. Melanie's mother had asked for a dishwasher ages ago, but her father didn't see the need to "waste" that much money. Of course, if they didn't keep the furnace blasting all winter, they might have the money they needed. Melanie wiped her brow and washed another fork. Once everything was cleaned up, they joined the men in the living room, where the conversation was on football.

"Nope," said Melanie's mother. "None of that tonight. We're going to talk about real things."

"Football is real," Thomas protested.

"Did anyone see *Meet the Mormons*?" Mom countered. "Such a great film. I'm sure it will bring thousands to the Church."

"I don't know why they didn't interview *me*," said Deidre. "I'm interesting, too. I won the prize for Best Cake at the county fair, and I'm only twenty-two years old. Plus, I came in third in that volleyball tournament."

Melanie didn't say anything, but she hardly thought third place in a stake volleyball tournament was worthy of film coverage.

The evening progressed with more unsatisfying conversation. How wonderful it was that the country might finally have another Republican for president. How there'd been three record low temperatures in Anchorage last week, so global warming was clearly just a liberal pretense to destroy the economy. How righteousness was winning back the country, evidenced by all the support to pass another Constitutional amendment outlawing abortion.

Melanie realized she was the only one in the room who found the discussion unsatisfying. The rest of her family seemed to feel their pathway to exaltation being validated by God Almighty.

Melanie did get the tuna, she reminded herself.

But then the conversation began to take an interesting turn toward the personal. After a few brief comments about the woman who'd just been sustained as first counselor in the ward Relief Society—"She's divorced but remarried in the temple"—some news about the stake president entered the discussion.

"Turns out he had an account with Ashley Madison," Dad said triumphantly. Melanie knew her father had never liked the man, after being snubbed for the position himself.

"Ashley Madison is old news," said Thomas, his brows furrowed. "Why is all this talk about adultery coming out now?"

Dad shrugged. "I guess there was a lot of data to sort through. And it's not like anyone besides us folks in Spanish Fork knows who he is. Took a while to realize this was news."

"Is he being excommunicated?" asked Melanie.

Dad shook his head. "He's claiming someone put the account in his name illegally." He kicked off his shoes, tossing them beside the sofa. "So no excommunication, but he'll be released. He's been in the position five years already anyway. The Church isn't going to announce the real reason for his release, of course. I just happen to know someone who knows someone." Then he grinned mischievously, putting his feet up on the coffee table. "And someone you all know and love may be getting a new calling soon."

"This is very disturbing," said Thomas.

Melanie couldn't resist making a comment. "I don't see what the big deal is," she said. "It's not as if Joseph Smith didn't have sex with other men's wives."

There was a horrified silence in the room. Perhaps Melanie wouldn't have to wait until she was married before no longer being forced to attend these family dinners.

"That—that was entirely different," Mom managed to get out. "An angel with a flaming sword *forced* him to do that."

"And he *married* all those other women," Deidre pointed out. "He wasn't committing adultery or anything."

"Well, that's good," Melanie replied. "I've been so worried about the dream I had last week." No one seemed to want to ask what she'd dreamed, so Melanie continued without being prompted. "I was on the Other Side, and Joseph Smith asked me to become his 35th wife." She was lying, of course, but reading the Church essays had made her want to sin so badly. She wondered how much longer she could stay.

"Did you really dream that?" Mom asked, breathless with excitement. Melanie nodded.

"Then you've finally passed your test," Dad said with a smile, leaning forward and scratching a toe. "We weren't sure you would."

"Now you don't have to get married," Mom added. The idea seemed to relieve her. But it wasn't as if twenty-six was ancient, Melanie thought.

"She can still get married," Thomas interjected. "Joseph can still take her." He smiled and looked at Deidre, who wasn't smiling back.

Melanie decided not to mention the abortions Joseph forced his polyamorous women to undergo. She'd had her fun. "So are you submitting any recipes for the new ward cookbook?" she asked Deidre.

"I'm not in your ward," Deidre said icily. "I can't submit."

The conversation limped along for another fifteen minutes, and then Melanie said she had to get back home. No one seemed to mind her being the first to leave. But when she opened the door, she stopped in her tracks. The snow was eight inches deep and falling fast. And there was a stiff wind. Melanie had forgotten about the snow, the house was so hot.

"Oh, dear," said Mom. "Looks like a blizzard. I knew I should have checked the weather today."

Deidre joined them by the door. "Oh, boy!" she said. "A sleepover!" Her mood had changed quickly, Melanie noticed. Since Melanie didn't really want children, she was thinking of having a hysterectomy and taking hormone supplements so she'd never have any more mood swings herself. She wanted to do something irrevocable. Something she couldn't be talked into repenting. Perhaps if she did enough inappropriate things, her family would stop asking her to visit altogether.

She'd always been taught the value of killing two birds with one stone.

Mom didn't look as pleased with this turn of events as Deidre did, and Melanie was none too happy about the snow, either. It was hardly 8:30, but she didn't think she could put up with her family's company a moment longer. Blizzards weren't *that* bad, she thought. And she only lived three miles away. She could practically walk home if she had to. It was only ten degrees. She'd been in colder weather.

Mom closed the door.

"I'm really beat," Melanie said. "Do you mind if I head straight to bed?"

"Take Dan and Hunter's room," Mom replied. "Deidre and Thomas will take yours and Deidre's."

"I love that room," said Deidre. "We should sleep over more often."

They all still lived within the city limits.

Melanie borrowed an emergency toothbrush, went in her brothers' bedroom, and stripped to her bra and panties. Since she hadn't served a mission or married yet, she didn't have to wear Mormon underwear. Good reasons not to ever serve a mission or get married, she thought. She pulled the covers up and tried to get to sleep. She'd probably have to miss work in the morning. At least some good would come from all this.

Though she wasn't particularly tired, Melanie eventually fell asleep, grateful for the oblivion. She awoke much later, though, as if she'd heard something. Straining, she could only hear silence. Everyone was clearly in bed. It was sure hot, though. Ever since watching *The Day After Tomorrow*, Melanie's mother had a pathological fear of being caught by a flash Ice Age and freezing to death in her sleep. She kept the house another two degrees warmer after everyone went to bed. Melanie tossed off the covers and tried to fall back asleep.

Sometime later, she stirred when she heard another noise. She opened her eyes and thought she saw something in the room. She almost yelled, but something told her to remain silent. She closed her eyes except for a slit and watched the figure approach the bed. It was a man, she could see now. Thomas. He was wearing only his garments.

What the hell was he doing in here, Melanie wondered? But then she saw. Thomas stood next to the bed and stared at her for several minutes. Melanie wondered if she could casually pull up the covers as if doing so in her sleep, but she was afraid Thomas wouldn't buy it. He tugged down the bottom half of his garments and started fondling himself.

Oh, my god.

What was she going to do? Confrontation seemed like the worst response. Everyone would surely blame her in any event. And Melanie didn't want to take a chance on how her brother-in-law might react if he felt threatened.

Melanie heard a slight sigh as Thomas came in his hand. She watched while he looked at his cupped palm, as if trying to decide what to do with the mess. He reached over and seemed about to touch her crotch with the stuff. Melanie was getting ready to scream when Thomas suddenly withdrew his hand and licked it instead.

Melanie thought she was going to be sick.

Thomas leaned over the bed and inhaled deeply. Then he turned and walked back out of the room.

Melanie would not be coming back for any more family dinners, snow or no snow, genealogy or no genealogy. She climbed out of bed, put her clothes back on, and looked out the window. Still coming down furiously.

She looked at the bedroom door. Surely, the danger was over for the evening, but she dragged a chair across the floor and set it against the doorknob. But that wasn't going to be good enough, she decided. She would sleep in the chair and add even more weight to the blockage. She tore a blanket off the bed and sat, covering herself to her chin.

It was so terribly, terribly hot, she thought, wiping sweat from her forehead. But she sat awake in the chair the rest of the night, shivering the entire time.

The Gathering 13

"Good grief, Emma," said Jon when she'd finished speaking. "That sounds like a story Quinn would tell. I was expecting something better from you."

"It's not really even a story, is it?" asked Nellie, examining a knot.

Emma looked as if she were about to speak. Then she looked at Quinn, closed her mouth, and for some reason turned to Gavin. "I've never told anyone about this before," she said, "but my brother used to fondle me." She blushed and turned her face downward. "He never actually…you know… but he did touch me several times."

Someone sighed. Gavin realized it was him.

"How old were you?" asked Jon. "I mean, some of that is natural childhood behavior."

Emma looked at him. "I was twelve and he was fifteen." Now Jon looked at a loss for words. "Is that the kind of thing you did with your sisters when you were fifteen?" Emma pressed.

Jon looked uncomfortable, and Quinn looked disgusted. But Jon didn't answer. Gavin looked at each of them in turn and then at Nellie, embroidering away as if a new runner meant anything. What was wrong with people? He hadn't even masturbated until he was sixteen, and then only a couple of times of year, stopping altogether when serving as a missionary. He'd picked up the habit again after returning to Utah, but even as naïve as he was, he knew how often some of his friends were beating off.

When he'd said to his bishop that he "only" touched himself once every six months, his bishop had replied, "How many times do you have to commit murder to be worthy of the death penalty?"

Gavin had continued to live in guilt the next few decades. Even now, when he woke up in the morning occasionally with an erection, he felt like he'd kissed Jesus in front of the Roman soldiers.

He did want to kiss Jesus, he thought.

Stop it!

Gavin couldn't decide if all people were repellant ogres, or if something about the way the Church handled normal human impulses forced those impulses to metamorphose into something else. He looked at Nellie, who'd apparently never had a stray sinful thought in her life. Unless you could count arrogance. Gavin wondered if the Mormon hierarchy of sins allowed serious personality flaws to go unchecked, the way a faithful Mormon could justify watching an R-rated movie. "There was a little violence, a few murders here and there, but there wasn't any sex."

"Jon doesn't molest anyone," said Gavin. "He just drowns puppies."

Everyone turned to look at him, and Gavin realized he'd said his thoughts out loud. He was about to apologize but then decided he didn't want to. Even Nellie was looking at him strangely. She turned back to her sewing and stared at the blue thread trailing from her needle. She started to put the runner aside but then pulled it back onto her lap and set her jaw firmly.

"Whoever's next better tell a goddamn inspirational story," she said through gritted teeth. "I'm getting sick of all this effing nonsense." She looked up as if daring anyone to comment on her language, which was clearly hers this time, and not some character's. She returned to her runner, and Jon raised his hand and started to speak.

Nourishing the Dead

"Bassel," said Detective Kirchmann, tapping the table with his index finger, "I'm afraid we'll need to go over it all again." Bassel felt the detective's eyes boring into him, but he remained calm. It wasn't as if he hadn't been in sticky situations once or twice before in his life. "There's something you're not telling me, and we'll stay here until you do."

Bassel smiled. "I've got all the time in the world, sir," he said calmly.

Detective Kirchmann closed his eyes, gritted his teeth a moment, and then smiled, but without humor. He looked at his watch. "What were you doing in the truck?" The man couldn't be more than thirty, thought Bassel. So ridiculously young to think he knew anything about life.

"Sayid, Firas, and I were immigrating to Germany," Bassel repeated for the tenth time.

"From where?"

"From Palmyra, as I said before."

"And how did you end up in Austria?" asked the detective.

Bassel sighed. He did in fact have all the time in the world, but legalities bored him enormously. They'd left

Europe altogether during the Inquisition. Now *those* were legalities. He and his colleagues usually tried to stay out of the limelight whenever possible. No interviews when they were the sole survivors of a plane crash, for instance. But they'd had no way of knowing the traffickers would leave them all locked up in the refrigerator car, abandoned on the side of the road for days.

"We just climbed in the truck with everyone else and paid our money. They said they could get us past all the borders."

Detective Kirchmann tapped the table with his finger. "I think *you* three are the traffickers, that you deliberately killed everyone. You're not going to be deported. You'll spend the rest of your life in prison in our country."

Bassel frowned. "When can I see my friends?"

"After you tell me what happened."

Bassel shook his head. Heavenly Father, he prayed silently, please help us out of this mess. Bassel, Sayid, and Firas had chosen to be smuggled out of Syria with the other sixty-nine refugees because they knew it meant being in close quarters for several days. They would have a captive audience as they preached. Who would have suspected that even at the moment of death, when Bassel promised them all life if they repented and accepted the gospel, they'd be so obstinate as to refuse to convert?

Even if he wouldn't have been able to deliver on his promise.

He remembered Sobibor. Not a single Jew had converted in all his time there. One gypsy had, but the man ended up recanting a mere ten days later. And was killed two days after that.

So close.

"The driver left us," said Bassel. "I've told you over and over."

"What happened to the others in the truck with you?"

Bassel shrugged. "You know what happened." He looked up at the light bulb hanging from the ceiling. "Everyone suffocated."

"Except you three," said Detective Kirchmann. "How do you explain that?"

Bassel couldn't very well tell him the truth. "My friends and I live at a higher elevation than most people in my country. We don't need as much oxygen."

The detective was recording the interview, but he was also writing notes as they talked. He wrote something now and then said, "Everyone else had been dead for three days by the time we opened the rear door. There'd been no oxygen back there for quite some time."

Bassel sighed. "We're alive, aren't we?" he said. "Of course there was oxygen."

"I think you three had just gone in the truck moments before we came along. That's what I think. Tell me why you went in and closed the door behind you."

"For the lovely aroma," Bassel said with a straight face. The feces and ammonia had been overwhelming long before the bodies began decomposing. Bassel rubbed his forehead, remembering the screams and the pounding for hours and hours before everyone finally became silent.

Something about it had been exciting.

He'd first noticed it during the Black Death in Italy. He was so envious of the Italians dying by the thousands around him.

People so close to death should be preparing to meet their Maker. But no Catholics back in Naples had converted during the plague. No Lamanites dying of smallpox converted. And no Syrians in the back of the refrigerator truck converted.

Bassel and his friends had been preaching for so long, for so many hundreds of years, ever since being blessed by Jesus that they could remain alive until his Second Coming. They'd traveled the world, learned five dozen different languages, preached to peoples in city and town, on farm and sea. And in all that time, they'd only brought fewer than five thousand people to the truth.

They didn't even average one a year each. Some years there was nothing at all. And they weren't stupid. They tried everything. They became priests, they became witch doctors, they became teachers, mayors, bartenders. They taught the sick, the elderly, the young. They tried every approach they could think of.

And in all that time, they watched three thousand of the five thousand converts fall away before their eventual death.

"You think this is funny?" the detective demanded.

Bassel shook his head.

"Why were you having sex with the dead woman?" the detective asked harshly.

How could Bassel possibly explain? He wanted to say he did it because he'd come to love these people in the short time they suffered together. He wanted to say that he could never stop hoping his seed would be powerful enough to raise the dead. Not make them immortal as he was, just bring them back for another normal lifespan. He'd been trying it with all the women he'd loved over the past few hundred years, ever since losing Mikka in the Aizu earthquake. It had never worked even once. But he was powerless to stop trying.

Sayid and Firas did the same thing these days. They'd finished having sex with all the dead women in the truck before the police opened the door, but Bassel was trying a second time with Sabeen. She was so lovely and sweet, even if deceived. And her sons Tarek and Ammar had been so well-behaved and intelligent.

He wanted to bring her back.

"That woman had been dead three days," Detective Kirchmann continued. "In a hot, crowded truck." He shook his head. "You are one sick animal. That's why I know you killed them all. So you could defile their bodies."

"It's not like that," Bassel protested. "Really."

"The DNA evidence will prove all three of you are guilty of necrophilia."

Bassel nodded. Perhaps he *was* a freak. One could grow tired of living. Grow to love death enough to make love to it.

When was Christ ever going to come back? It had been the Last Days for so long. Bassel wasn't sure he could take much more of this. You'd think Jesus could come visit once in a while, offer a little sustenance. But they'd been on their own ever since their anointing.

"Your friends have already confessed," the detective said. "There's no point denying it any longer."

Bassel smiled. He was certainly aware of this kind of manipulation, had practiced it himself hundreds of times over the years. The tried and true "Good Nephite, Bad Nephite." But maybe he should stop fighting and just go along with it. He was so tired. So very, very tired. Perhaps they'd put him in solitary confinement. Then Heavenly Father couldn't possibly expect him to preach any longer.

"Yes," he said. "I killed them. I killed them all. My friends had nothing to do with it. It was all my idea."

Detective Kirchmann smiled, still without humor. "That's the exact same thing both of them said, too."

Bassel spent the next hour with the detective, first filming and then writing out and signing his confession. After that, he was led to a cell where he was finally reunited again with Sayid and Firas. He could hardly remember his real name, he'd changed it so many times over the years. The door shut and the three men hugged, but no one said a word. They sat on a bench next to one another, holding hands silently. Bassel knew these men better than Jesus did. Better than Heavenly Father. He sat on the right end of the bench and squeezed Sayid's hand.

Maybe they could lift weights in the gym. Or read books. Or work in the laundry. Anything not to have to preach any longer.

But if they'd had to preach in the Soviet gulags, they'd certainly have to preach here. Bassel shook his head sadly.

"It's going to be all right," Firas said.

"Of course it will." Sayid nodded.

"We may get beaten up a lot," said Bassel. "Get knifed or something." All so pointless.

"It's not America," Firas replied. "Besides, it's not like we haven't gone through that dozens of times already."

They were silent a few more minutes. Bassel wondered what they might have for dinner. It had been days since they'd eaten. Being immortal didn't mean one never grew hungry.

"Hey!" Firas said suddenly. Bassel and Sayid turned to him. "We may have to *make* people beat us up."

"Why in the world would we do that?" asked Bassel. Pain was still pain, immortal body or not. Well, not immortal exactly. But nearly so. They still had to be changed in the twinkling of an eye when they were resurrected after the Second Coming. Then they'd truly be immortal.

What in heaven's name could be worse than immortality, Bassel wondered?

"Don't you see?" Firas continued. "If we get all beat up, and then we *forgive* the people who beat us, we might be able to bring some of them to the gospel." He smiled. "Maybe this whole thing was just to get us to the right people."

Bassel looked at Firas, and then he looked at Sayid. And he suddenly knew that if he spent one single day longer with either of them he would apostatize from the truth himself.

"We'll be behind bars for two decades or more," Bassel said wearily. "No women for twenty years. Not even any dead women." He knew he would have to do something he'd never done before, not in two thousand years. He would have to start killing people himself. And even if they were men, he'd have to try to nourish them back to life with his seed. How could God stand being alive forever? Even just two millennia was driving Bassel mad. All he wanted to do was surround himself with death. Those three days in the parked truck had been the best time he'd had in years.

Well, that Ebola outbreak a couple of years ago hadn't been too bad. He tried to remember the stench. He closed his eyes and breathed deeply.

"You okay, Bassel?" asked Sayid.

Bassel looked at Sayid, and Sayid's brows furrowed in concern at what he saw. His friend pulled away and held onto Firas's hand tightly. Firas clung onto Sayid in return. So immature, even at their age. Bassel walked up to the door and peered through the tiny window into the hallway. He saw a guard walk by leading another prisoner, and he giggled. Then he turned back to his friends and giggled and giggled and giggled. They looked at him in horror, but all he could do was laugh.

The Gathering 14

"Oh, my heck," Emma said when Jon finished speaking. "And I actually let you touch me last night."

"What's with all the Three Nephite stories?" asked Gavin.

Jon shrugged. "You can't help but think of them at times like this. This is what they've been waiting for every day of their lives for two thousand years."

"But why did you tell such a sick story?" asked Quinn. She was rocking the baby, who'd been crying for the past five minutes, as if she somehow sensed the negative energy in the room and was protesting. Even after such a brief time, Gavin was ready to put the child outside on the doorstep and let her fend for herself. He wasn't sure Jon was altogether wrong in assuming that prolonged exposure to humans could turn even saints into monsters.

Nellie stood up without a word with her yellow plastic glass grasped tightly in her hand and headed to the kitchen for a refill. But as Gavin watched her walk off, he saw her pause halfway down the hallway, lean again the wall, and put her hand to her head as if exhausted. She was clearly under a lot of pressure, just from the Apocalypse alone, much less from hosting a houseful of sinful survivors. Gavin thought he should feel sorry for her and was a little disappointed he didn't. Maybe, he thought hopefully, she finally understood what it was like for him to feel this amount of pressure every single day of his life.

Only she wouldn't, would she, Gavin realized. People never made those kinds of connections. She wouldn't feel his years of pain just because she now understood pain herself, any more than he felt her pain today, though he'd had decades already of understanding what pain was.

God was right to destroy the world. Gavin wondered why he'd waited this long. Out of a perverse desire to inflict suffering himself?

Nellie walked back to the living room a few moments later, and Gavin watched as she sat down. He waited to catch her eye and forced a smile when he did. She looked at him blankly for a long moment and then took a sip of her water. He wanted nothing more than to pee in her cup.

He realized with a deep rush of sadness he wasn't going to make it. Not even if he was still alive at the end. He looked at Emma and Jon holding hands, and Quinn tickling her baby's foot.

And Gavin knew what story he needed to tell next. But before he could tell it, Quinn began a story of her own.

Honeymoon in New Orleans

"Feel that breeze," Morganella said, lifting her face into the wind at their bedroom window, her long blond hair flowing gently behind her. She closed her eyes in ecstasy. It had been so unbearably hot earlier. The change in weather was a godsend.

"I told you we'd have a good time in New Orleans," said Theo. He leaned over and kissed her on the cheek. There had been a lot of ecstasy since they'd arrived the day before.

"Still seems like an odd place for Mormons to spend their honeymoon," Morganella returned. She'd wanted to go to Branson, Missouri, or to Nauvoo, or to see the dedication of the temple in Newport Beach. This place, with all its jazz music and people sucking crawfish heads, just seemed a bit decadent.

She thought about sucking crawfish heads.

"You didn't enjoy the beignets earlier?" Theo asked teasingly. "You didn't enjoy the jambalaya?"

Morganella stuck her tongue out at her husband. "The last thing I want to do is feel fat on my honeymoon," she replied.

"I need to eat something low calorie." She thought about sucking again, but not crawfish heads.

"We'll walk all over the Aquarium tomorrow and get some exercise," Theo said. "And the day after, we'll go to the Battle of New Orleans monument in Chalmette."

"No," Morganella said, pulling Theo close to her. "We bought all that food at Schwegmann's. And all that Barq's rootbeer. We're staying in our room the entire day tomorrow and not coming out for anything." She gently rubbed her right nipple through her blouse.

"All day?" asked Theo with a smile. "It's only taking me twenty minutes from start to finish. All day is a long time."

"I've been waiting for you since before your mission," Morganella reminded him. "If we have sex fifteen times tomorrow, it won't be enough for me."

"Fifteen times!" Theo looked both shocked and excited by the prospect.

Morganella was a little shocked herself. Even thinking about sex at all had been a mortal sin only a week ago. And now she was free to think—and act—on her desires as often as she wished. She reached over and grabbed Theo's crotch through his jeans. He grew hard in seconds.

How wonderful not to be sinning any more when she felt this way.

"Shall I shut the window?" asked Theo, reaching for the grip on the lower pane. "Someone might hear us." He grinned. "I plan to be noisy."

Morganella shook her head. "This Bed and Breakfast was advertised especially for honeymooners. No one around here's going to care." She unzipped Theo's pants. "In fact, after all those years of having to cover my shoulders, I want to be as carefree as possible. This is supposed to be the City That Care Forgot."

"I told you we'd have a good time in New Orleans."

Morganella kneeled in front of her husband and took his member into her mouth. Members were good things, she thought. That's why the Church always referred to its followers that way. She took Theo's as far down her throat as she could. Her mother had told her she might gag, but she was so excited she wished *she* had a member of her own to become engorged.

She couldn't help but remember that New Orleans was also supposed to be the Big Easy.

Morganella and Theo spent Saturday night in New Orleans in their bedroom, trying sex in two new different ways. Finally, around three in the morning, they fell asleep in each other's arms.

There was a knock on the door in the morning, but Theo put his hand over Morganella's mouth and shook his head. The knocking continued for a couple more minutes and then stopped. Theo smiled and reached down to slowly insert his finger inside his wife. Ah, to wake up to such feelings, thought Morganella. Eternity as gods meant they could spend every morning for the next billion years like this. It was worth a few years of celibacy and strict chastity to be awarded this prize.

Though she had to admit, the prying questions during interviews with her bishop had been unpleasant. Especially when the bishop was her uncle. "Do you masturbate?" he asked her during every worthiness interview. "What kinds of sexual thoughts do you have?" "Do you ever have sex dreams? What kind of sex do you have in your dreams?" The questions had begun when she was twelve and continued up until last week. At least these days, the bishop was her father's boss at work. He asked lots of questions about how she inserted her tampons.

But she'd passed all her interviews, even with the stake president. She'd made it to the temple. She was sealed for time and all eternity to this wonderful, wonderful man. Whose throbbing penis was sliding into her right now.

She knew what Celestial life was going to be like, and it was good.

They finished their first round of sex for the day, ate a leisurely breakfast in their room, brushed their teeth, showered, and started all over again. Their bodies fresh and clean, they began exploring each other with their noses and tongues, in places Morganella had never thought about. Much. Theo came in three different orifices. Morganella stood or knelt in a different position for each one. By the time night fell, they were both so sore they weren't sure they could continue. Even resting between rounds, they were both exhausted and a bit raw.

Morganella had been so worried they wouldn't know what to do. The two of them had never even allowed themselves to discuss the subject. But now they were free.

Free! And it was as if the Veil had been parted, and all knowledge bestowed upon them.

She'd never even considered the possibility of her husband swallowing his own semen, but after he came inside her this morning, he inserted a finger, grabbed some of the stuff back, and licked it off his finger. Who needed sex talks? Who needed pornography? The Spirit was telling them everything they needed to know.

All they'd needed to do was follow the rules for a few years, and now the whole world was theirs.

"What say we call it a night?" Theo suggested, leaning back on the bed. A gust of wind rattled the window, and he laughed. "Even Mother Nature knows when we've been behaving too naturally." He touched Morganella's arm gently.

"It's only 9:00," Morganella protested. "How can we go to bed this early on our honeymoon? And in New Orleans?"

"It's Sunday," Theo answered.

Morganella couldn't bring herself to admit out loud she was tired, too. It was a pleasant exhaustion, the way a person might feel after a long run, or picking apples all day for the poor at the Church welfare farm. "All right," she said, "you win. But I just need a little more semen before I go to sleep."

Theo laughed. "I ran out a few hours ago. I've been mostly shooting blanks ever since."

"Well, I want *something*. Let me put your balls in my mouth again."

"Be my guest."

Morganella fell asleep with Theo's testicles in her mouth, the bedside lamp still on. Theo was in no position to protest, though, as he'd fallen asleep as well. Morganella eventually rolled over, the balls flopping out of her mouth, and Theo murmured in his sleep. Around 6:00 in the morning, the lights went out. Morganella had to go pee, and she stumbled to the bathroom.

The wind was rather strong outside. She flipped the light switch several times, to no avail. She shook Theo. "Wake up, honey."

He smiled sleepily at her. "Morning, sunshine."

"No, Theo," she replied. "There's no sunshine. I think we're in trouble."

His eyes slowly focused. "What's wrong?"

"The weather is really bad." Morganella vaguely remembered hearing a couple of days ago about a "storm" headed their way but hadn't thought much of it. "We have to get dressed and ask the B&B owners what's going on."

They dressed quickly in the dim light and walked down the hall to the kitchen. No one was there. No one was in the common living room, either. Morganella began knocking on the other two bedroom doors. No one answered.

Theo drew back the curtain in the living room. The wind was ripping leaves and small branches off the trees in front of the house. A garbage can rolled along the sidewalk, and an old pizza box flew by. The front door was rattling. Rain poured down outside and lightning flashed viciously. Thunder vibrated throughout the building. "The street has an inch or two of water," said Theo.

"What should we do?" Morganella asked calmly. Her husband held the priesthood. He would have the answers.

He shrugged. "We still have food in our room. This will probably blow over in a few hours."

Morganella opened the refrigerator. "Let's eat whatever might spoil," she said. "Ooh, look, strawberries!"

Theo laughed. "Can I place them all over your body and eat them off you?"

"I go first," she replied. She wanted to place six strawberries in Theo's butt crack and dig her face into his ass. She had no idea why that sounded like fun. It had never even been a fantasy before. Not that she had allowed herself to fantasize very often. After she ate Theo's berries, she would then insert a few pieces of the red fruit halfway into her vagina and make Theo cram his face into her as well.

Celestial marriage was wonderful.

After breakfast, they started to have sex on the sofa as the wind buffeted the house. Since no one was home, they moved to the kitchen table to finish. Not quite as fun as it sounded, but something to write about in their journals.

Several hours later, the winds started dying down. "I think it's over," said Theo.

"A hurricane in New Orleans," Morganella said, giggling. "At least we'll have something G-rated we can talk to our families about when they ask how things went."

There was no television, and if there was a radio in the house, they couldn't find it. Morganella and Theo spent a few hours talking about stories from Church history. At first, the change in topic worried Morganella—was the honeymoon over?—but all throughout their talking, Theo caressed her arms, legs, breasts, and stomach, and she kept her hands roving over his irresistible body parts the entire time as well.

Since their ancestors had both crossed the plains into Salt Lake, they'd heard these stories their entire lives, and it felt comfortable to fall back into them. Theo particularly liked Parley P. Pratt's escape from jail. Morganella enjoyed talking about the tradition of funeral potatoes. Theo talked about the tarring and feathering of Joseph Smith. Morganella recounted the story of the heavens opening up at the Kirtland temple.

"And who can forget the faith and dedication of the members when they donated their best china and glassware to be crushed and applied to the exterior walls, to make the temple glisten in the sun?" Mormons had such a rich history. She and Theo would pass it on to their children, and their children's children.

She was glad they weren't using condoms or pills. Righteous Mormon newlyweds started their families right away.

Morganella had dozed off, her head on Theo's shoulder, when suddenly Theo stood up without warning and shouted. "There's water in the house!"

Morganella looked about. Almost an inch of water covered the floor. "The rain stopped a few hours ago," she said. "I don't understand."

"Pull your feet up," Theo demanded. "That water's probably contaminated."

Morganella looked around the room. "We're in a one-story house," she said. "There's nowhere to go."

Theo pulled his feet up onto the sofa as well, but only fifteen minutes later, the water was a foot deep. He stood and trudged through the water, looking up at the ceiling. "There!" he said a few minutes later, pointing upward to the ceiling in front of one of the bedrooms.

"What is it?"

"A way to get to the attic." Theo dragged the kitchen table through the water and placed it underneath the square panel in the ceiling. Then he carried a kitchen chair over and set it on the table. The water was three feet deep now. By the time they pulled themselves up into the attic, it was over four feet deep.

A couple of magazines and throw pillows floated in the water. Morganella noticed some packaged condoms floating as well. She remembered the B&B supplied them free for honeymooners.

For sinners.

"How deep is the water going to get?" asked Morganella, frowning. "And why is it flooding? There's no rain."

Theo shrugged. "Maybe coming to New Orleans wasn't such a good idea. God has to destroy this wicked place sometime."

"But we never went to Bourbon Street," Morganella protested. "We never had a sip of alcohol."

Theo bit his lip and looked down through the attic opening into the rising water below. "Do you think," he said softly, "do you think maybe having *that* much sex was still a sin?" He looked at Morganella, and she instinctively covered her breasts with her hands.

"It's a trial," she replied. "Heavenly Father always tries those he loves."

There was no light in the attic, and the dim light from the living room was growing dimmer as the dusk slowly turned into night. The water was still rising. By the time they could feel the water enter the attic, it was pitch black. "Morganella, what are we going to do?"

Morganella couldn't believe her ears. The priesthood holder was supposed to be in charge. She tried to bang on the roof, to see if she could loosen any boards, but there were nails poking through from where the shingles had been attached.

"Fuck me," she said. She wasn't sure if that came across as an instruction or consternation.

"Morganella…"

"Do it," she demanded again.

There wasn't even enough to room to stand erect, but her back wasn't what Morganella needed to be erect right now. Theo shoved himself inside her, more roughly than he ever had before. She held onto the rafters to keep from being knocked over, her head bumping against the roof with each thrust, a nail digging into her scalp. They both shouted as he came inside her.

She was pregnant now. She could tell. And one day, she'd tell the baby how she was conceived. When she was on her way to her own temple wedding. It would be a story of great faith.

The water was halfway up their calves. "I'm going to swim for help," said Theo.

"You can't!" Morganella held onto Theo's arm. "You can't see your way out of the house."

"Once I'm outside, I'll climb up on the rooftop and tap to let you know I've made it. I'll try to pull off the shingles and some boards. But if I can't, I'll get help."

"Oh, Theo."

Theo fumbled for Morganella in the dark and kissed her. "Let's pray," he said. He offered a beautiful, sweet prayer, kissed her once more, and dropped through the attic opening back into the house below. The Lord would protect them, she told herself. They had been so good.

Morganella counted slowly to sixty. Then she counted to sixty again. And once more. After five minutes had passed, she figured she'd been counting too quickly and started over. By the time five more minutes had passed, the water was up to her chest, and because of the way the slanting roof forced her to lean over, her face was only inches above her chest. Soon the water was touching her lips.

"O Lord, my God!"

She began crying.

"I'll confess everything to the bishop!" she called out into the darkness. She'd made a horrific miscalculation. Sex was perhaps acceptable after marriage, but it was never to be enjoyed. Maybe in the Celestial Kingdom, but certainly not here on Earth. She'd made a terrible, terrible mistake. "If you let me live, I'll tell the bishop everything I've done the past few days. Every last detail. I'll be a good girl again. Please, Heavenly Father. Please!"

She leaned her head backward, trying to keep her nose up as high as it would go, waiting to hear Theo tap on the roof outside. She kept straining to hear, straining desperately in the blackness. But the waters covered her ears the same time it covered her nose.

The Gathering 15

"Being raped gave you a very warped view of sex," Emma said when Quinn finished.

Quinn shrugged. "I certainly got my warped view from somewhere," she admitted. Harper was asleep in her lap, and she caressed the baby's head gently. "I've never told anyone this," she added hesitantly, "not even the bishop, but…"

Was it possible for personal revelations to be any more personal than the stories they were already telling, Gavin wondered?

"Yes?" asked Emma, leaning slightly in Quinn's direction.

"I love my baby," she replied. "But I hate her, too. Every time I look at her, I see the creep who attacked me." She paused. "And I can't help but think about the articles I've read discussing DNA. How much of our personality is shaped by the way we're raised, and how much of it is determined by genetics?" She shook her head. "What if my baby grows up to be a horrible person?"

"We all worry about that," said Emma. Then she grew quiet, clearly thinking about her own children she'd just lost. Gavin thought about his son who'd turned out to be a lot like him, and his daughters who had turned out to be a lot like Nellie.

"The only thing we have control over," said Jon, "is to raise our children in the Church."

"Or during the Apocalypse," said Gavin.

Nellie snorted. "My husband. Always the optimist. Why not think about raising your children in the Millennium? Emma, you'll have yours back in no time."

"I want them back *now*," she returned.

"So they can suffer with the rest of us? They're much better off where they are."

Emma stood up and threw her blue cup at Nellie. The last of her water sprayed out across the carpet. "My kids are *not* better off dead!" she said.

Nellie looked completely shocked. "I just meant…" she began. "I just meant…" She stood up wearily and moved to the window, pulling the curtain aside slightly. "The Franklins' house down the street is burning," she stated calmly.

"Who fuckin' cares?" said Emma.

Nellie looked at her, seemed to be thinking of a response, and then appeared to think better of it. She peered through the window again and then pulled the curtain shut once more. Gavin knew that what he was about to say would hurt Nellie's feelings, but he couldn't bring himself to care about that anymore. Perhaps it wasn't only the world that was ending. He cleared his throat and began speaking.

My TBM Husband

"Ugh," I said. "90 degrees again today."

"I think this will be the 12ᵗʰ day this summer Seattle has had temperatures over 90 degrees," said Ken. "Before this year, even in our hottest years, we never had more than nine days that warm."

"At least it's going down to 80 for the rest of the week. That's good."

Ken shook his head. "No, it isn't, Lowell. 80 is hot, too."

"It's better than 90."

"*I'm* the one who's always pointing out relativity," he said. "You always just bitch."

"So maybe you're the one with the negative attitude today," I returned.

"Or maybe you're just being Pollyanna."

I looked at him. We weren't bantering. Ken and I had been married two years, ever since marriage became legal for us in Washington State. We'd been together twenty-eight years. Almost from the moment of marriage, though, he'd started becoming increasingly distant. Now he was picking a fight over nothing, something he'd been doing a lot more lately.

"In other words," I said, "if I bitch, I'm the bad guy. And if I don't bitch, I'm the bad guy. Interesting."

"I'm just saying that 80 degrees is still unnaturally warm for Seattle."

"I'm the one who donates to all the conservation groups," I pointed out. "I'm the one who took a bus down to Portland this week to support the protest against Shell."

Ken turned the TV from the Weather Channel back to Melissa Harris-Perry. We watched a segment on the American dentist who'd paid $50,000 to kill a protected lion in Zimbabwe. "The rich get away with everything," Ken muttered.

While I was grateful he'd found a different target for his criticism, I was still irritated. One of the things that had attracted me to Ken all those years ago was the fact that we could discuss so many different topics. While he was a carpenter, he was smarter and better educated than most of the bankers I worked with every day.

Ken seemed to sense he'd upset me, though he didn't appear to know why, so he went to the kitchen to wash the breakfast dishes. Sunday mornings were the only time these days we ate breakfast together. He cooked turkey bacon, grits, and eggs from our free range chickens out back. We owned almost three quarters of an acre in south Seattle, the land worth more than the house, which needed a new roof. We had to lock up the chickens at night because of the neighborhood raccoons, but they roamed freely most of the day.

Ken cooked the few meals we ate together, and I washed the dishes. Last night had been Date Night, but Ken had missed it to attend a function at the Liberty Socialist Hall, so I'd had a protein shake and a can of green beans. My weight had gone from 165 pounds to 210 over the last couple of decades. Ken was still around 175, where he'd been the day we met.

I'd been irritated about Date Night, but I left a card on Ken's desk for him when he came home, trying to be supportive. "You are my rock," it said.

Ken had thanked me unenthusiastically and then said, "I'm sorry you feel that way. I can't imagine what kind of rock you think I am."

"You're my seer stone," I replied with a grin.

Ken groaned. "I hate it when you talk about Mormons."

I did volunteer proofreading for Zarahemla Books. They were a small publisher specializing in "edgy" but "faith-promoting" Mormon fiction. They'd recently published a trilogy about black Mormons in the early Church. None of the books in their catalog were edgy enough for me, but I appreciated the effort to push the envelope at least slightly.

I also proofread for Sunstone magazine. Their articles were a little more progressive, but even they were pretty cautious. Ken thought I should forget about the Church completely, but I felt if there was ever going to be progress, it had to come from somewhere. Ken didn't believe in making things better incrementally. If something didn't work, it should be tossed out so one could start over right away.

Did that include me? Ken's attitudes about a lot of things had started changing since he joined the Party two years ago.

I went to the kitchen. "Thanks for washing the dishes."

"Sure."

He dried his hands and passed me on the way to his office at the back of the house. The room was a poorly built addition from the 1950's, the house itself built in 1910. Ken's office wasn't insulated, and even at 9:00 in the morning, it was starting to warm up. I stood at the edge of the kitchen and watched him sit at his desk. He turned on the computer and started playing Solitaire.

I walked back through the house, turning off the TV and going to my office in the front. I checked my emails, pretty much my only contact with other humans outside of work. A friend in Salt Lake talked about the sessions at the annual Sunstone symposium he'd attended the past couple of days. Another friend in San Francisco, a woman I'd met at an ex-Mormon conference several years ago, said she and her husband were replastering the walls of their living room and wouldn't have time to write for the next couple of weeks.

A disabled friend in New Orleans said she heard helicopters and lots of loud explosions the night before and called 9-1-1, but it turned out someone was just filming a movie. She was upset because the noise scared the stray cats away that she liked to feed.

Reading their emails was like drinking a caffeinated Coke, a sin I'd enjoyed even back when I was a believing Mormon. I could feel myself calming down as I got my fix of communication, though the experience was over within a mere two minutes. There were no other emails. Unless you counted the sixteen political messages I deleted unread. One could only sign just so many petitions that politicians were going to ignore in any event.

I checked my blood sugar. There were only two fingers that didn't hurt when I pricked them, but you couldn't only prick those same two fingers every day. Today I had to prick one that hurt. The sugar was 136. Not bad right after a meal.

I stared at my computer screen. Weekends were my only freedom from a suffocating job at the credit union. I was an equity loan processor, and the goal assigned me was to process at least 1.5 million in loans each month. This month, my underwriter and I had funded over 4 million. Our boss was so impressed she said she might have to ask about getting us each a $5 Starbucks gift card.

I came home exhausted every day, too tired to take the walks I knew I needed to lose weight. On weekends, I walked to the grocery store twenty-five minutes away and bought some groceries for the coming week, coming back to the house by bus. Ken's truck had broken down two weeks ago, so although he usually picked me up from the grocery, I was now carrying a case of protein shakes home on the bus, with other minimal supplies.

I had $56 left in my checking account. Ken had only contributed $85 last month to the household bills, and with his truck repair looming, he certainly wouldn't be contributing anything this month, either. My credit card was almost maxed out, paying for the bills Ken wouldn't pay.

He seemed to be getting fewer jobs lately, though the economy was improving. I couldn't tell if it was bad luck, personal choice, or something even worse.

I heard Ken in the kitchen getting some water. Then I heard him walk back to his office.

I headed to the back of the house, too. Ken was still playing Solitaire. "Wanna do anything today?" I asked.

"I've got to go over to Diane's and finish working on her deck," he said, still looking at the screen. "Then I've got to bike over to the Hall and do some work."

"Okay."

"What are you going to do?"

"Probably sit in front of the fan and listen to music."

"Must be nice."

I walked back to my office. Two days ago had been payday, and I'd made my student loan payment, a credit card payment, and paid the gas and internet bills. Ken's health insurance premiums came right out of my check.

God only knew what the gas bill would be next month. Friday morning I'd woken up at 4:00 to go pee, and I'd found one of the burners on the stove turned to about 70% of full, gas spewing into the air for at least six hours before I noticed. Fortunately, the windows were all open because of the heat. I debated whether or not to tell Ken when I got home from work, but then as I left at 6:00, I discovered the front door had been unlocked all night.

I went to bed by 9:00 every evening, and Ken stayed up two or three hours later, watching TV. He also went outside a couple of times to smoke. And he'd left the door unlocked. Sometimes when I came home from work, Ken would be gone, but I'd find both the front and back doors unlocked. Once, I'd even found the back door wide open. No one had come in. Ken had just forgotten to close the door.

Would I have enough money to cover all the care necessary if Ken was developing dementia? I wondered if I had the strength to stay with him if that was indeed the case. Or the desire.

Friday evening when I got home, I mentioned the gas and the door.

"I know, I know," said Ken. "I'm always doing something wrong."

I stared at my computer again and logged onto Facebook. I clicked Like for several quotes by Bernie Sanders, a couple by Robert Reich, and one by Elizabeth Warren. I shared a post someone had already posted about the *Deseret News* panning *The Book of Mormon Musical*, even though the reviewer admitted he hadn't seen the play. I scrolled down and saw an article about the first Native American woman who was now a federal judge. I clicked Like for that, too.

I never said much on Facebook, limiting my action mostly to liking things. Usually, the only way anyone else on Facebook interacted with me was also by liking a post I'd shared. Once, about two years ago, a former professor had IM'ed me, thinking back on some of his favorite students from his career. I'd IM'ed back, and that had been the end of that.

I read a defense now of the killing of the Zimbabwe lion posted by my cousin, who'd lived for a while in South Africa after meeting a returned missionary from Johannesburg online. I found it interesting that the few Mormons I kept in touch with always seemed to be on the wrong side of almost every issue.

They posted arguments against regulations to keep guns out of the hands of the mentally ill. They posted arguments against taking down the Confederate flag. They posted against food stamps for the poor. They posted against diplomacy with Iran, preferring war instead. They posted memes declaring that "Police Lives Matter" and "White Lives Matter," as if those positions were ever in question and needed defending.

One former mission colleague posted a photo of George W. Bush hugging a soldier, with the caption, "A Commander-in-Chief who *cares* about the military," clearly implying that Obama didn't care about those who served. I so wanted to reply, "You mean Bush, the guy who sent soldiers to die in an unjustified war that *he* started in the first place?" but I knew it was pointless to debate with TBMs.

True Blue Mormons said the most preposterous things. One had quoted Vladimir Putin a few days ago, spouting vehement disdain for minorities in his country, my former friend saying it was a shame when a Russian leader spoke the truth more than an American leader did. Two former mission colleagues and my niece spoke glowingly of Donald Trump.

Was I ever that awful back when I was a Mormon, I wondered?

I read a post from a former non-Mormon classmate who was studying poison dart frogs in Central America. She was a chemistry professor now, posing with two of her students in the jungle, all three smiling broadly.

I looked at some pictures of pretty flowers, some lenticular clouds over Mt. Rainier, an orca in the Sound.

I stared at a picture of a napping dog for a long time.

I heard Ken go in the bathroom and pee, and I walked to the back of the house. "Gotta head out," he said. "See you later."

"I can walk to the store again if you like. Anything you want for dinner?"

"How about salad?"

"Well, we have salad. I bought some yesterday."

He gave me a kiss and then headed down the stairs to the basement. He grabbed his bike and left through the basement door. I listened until I heard it latch behind him.

I sat on the sofa in front of the fan and turned on Pandora. Somehow, their algorithm had decided I liked Spanish music, though I hadn't entered any Spanish or Latino singers in my list of preferences. But to be honest, I found I *did* like most of the Spanish songs they played and listened for the next several minutes to the peaceful music as I stared at a three-foot-by-three-foot photograph of a live oak tree on my wall.

It drove Ken crazy to see me "wasting" time, but I had so much sensory overload during the week listening to my coworkers bicker incessantly that all I wanted to do on weekends was relax.

"Listen to the Rhythm of the Falling Rain" was playing now. I hit Like.

My whole life was about liking or not liking what others were deciding for me.

I closed my eyes and began fantasizing about winning the lottery and quitting my job, giving half to Ken to donate to whatever causes he wanted, and giving my own money to groups supporting single-payer healthcare and prison reform and wave energy and planting trees. I'd given twenty dollars last month to a guy who was writing a gay Mormon comic book called "Stripling Warrior."

I woke up later as a Carpenters song began playing and turned off the TV. I wiped the sweat from my forehead and listened to the fan whirring beside me.

I thought about the disaster last Wednesday evening when all the tension that had been growing between Ken and me since he'd joined the Liberty Socialist Party two weeks before our wedding came bursting out. We'd both been progressive Democrats before that. I'd been more critical of Obama than Ken had been. But now, there was nothing any Democrat could do that he would see in a positive light.

"Hillary's being controlled by the big banks," he said as we watched a Rachel Maddow segment on Wednesday.

"But Bernie isn't," I said. "He says all the right things."

"Hillary *says* the right things, too," Ken pointed out.

"Hillary has a track record that speaks against what she claims her positions are now. But Bernie has a thirty-year track record of actually *doing* the right things."

"He's not a real Socialist," Ken insisted.

"So you're not voting for him?" I asked.

"I only vote for people who are against Capitalism."

I tried breathing calmly and counting to myself but couldn't keep my mouth shut. "Ken," I said, "Bernie Sanders isn't perfect, but I don't think God is running. Neither is Trotsky. Bernie hasn't actually said anything you disagree with. He just hasn't approached some of the other topics you wish he would address. But someone who is right on 95% of the issues is still better than letting someone who is right on only 50% of the issues get the nomination. And it's sure a hell of a lot better than letting a Republican who is right on only 4% of the issues win."

"The worse things get, the more likely there will finally be a revolution."

"You're just like a Mormon who thinks the sooner the Apocalypse comes, the sooner Jesus will reign, so let's do what we can to start World War III."

Ken stared at me in shock. I should have let it stop at that, but my frustrations kept pouring out.

"You and I used to have School Night every Monday when we would watch a lecture together on DVD. Now you spend every Monday night at the Hall studying Communism.

We used to have Game Night on Thursdays and play Backgammon, but now every Thursday you're with your Socialist friends in an Exec meeting or branch meeting or some other meeting. I bought you the book *Capital* by Thomas Piketty, but you won't read it because it isn't endorsed by the Party.

"You hated tracting when we were missionaries in Berlin, but now you go door to door selling subscriptions of the Party newspaper. You won't study the candidates for local elections and make up your own mind. You wait until the Party issues its endorsements and vote for whoever they say." I paused while Ken stared at me with an increasingly huge frown. "You've become a TBM again. It's just that now you have a new religion."

I'd wondered if his obsession was a sign of the dementia I feared. But there were lots of fanatics out there with sound minds.

Though I suppose that was debatable.

Ken didn't even respond. He just stood and walked out of the house. I waited until 10:00 before finally going to bed. He still wasn't in when I woke up in the morning. I read about the Greenpeace protest in Portland on the internet and called in sick so I could ride down and offer what little support I could. I watched for hours in the 100-degree heat as protestors hung from a bridge blocking the ship trying to carry machinery necessary for drilling to the Arctic.

Ken couldn't even find it in himself to say anything positive about that. "There will never be any real change in how we treat the environment until we get rid of Capitalism."

I had gone to my office then and read my emails. One from a friend in West Hollywood complaining about all the new high rises being built in his neighborhood, and his fear of losing his rent-controlled apartment.

And lots of political emails.

There was no one else to talk to. I went back out to the living room, and Ken and I watched an episode of *The Walking Dead.*

I sighed. The whirring fan didn't seem to cool me down very much, but it was drying my eyes out. I got up from the sofa and went to the kitchen. A cold diet soda would feel soothing right now, but I hadn't been up to carrying a case of soda home on the bus, so there was nothing in the refrigerator other than my protein shakes, and I couldn't drink five of those a day. I poured a glass of tepid water from the faucet. Three fruit flies flittered away.

I put a can of sliced peaches in the fridge so it would be cold in time for dessert later.

I noticed Ken had left the bread bag open, the bread growing stale in the air. I closed the bag. Then I picked up the wrapper of a granola bar he'd left on the counter and threw it in the trash. How many more years of this? I closed my eyes and breathed deeply.

It would be hours yet before Ken came home, and I couldn't nap the entire day away. I put in a DVD of *Pride.* We'd watched it on Netflix several months ago, but I'd wanted to own a copy myself. Ken felt that a very Capitalist attitude, so I never told him I ordered it, slipping it onto my DVD shelf when he wasn't looking. I watched the movie occasionally while he was away. The story of gay activists supporting the striking miners inspired me every time.

When it was over, I turned off the TV and looked again at the fan whirring beside me. The air it blew was hot.

"God," I said aloud, looking at the live oak tree on the wall, "if you're really there, please help us all."

I put on my shoes, grabbed my bus card, and walked a block over to the bus stop. Fifteen minutes later, the 7 came by, and I climbed aboard. I sat on the raised seats in the middle of the bus and looked about at the other passengers. Mostly blacks, half of them native to America and the other half immigrants. There were several Asians, a few Latinos, and the odd white person. One of the white people was sitting right in front of me. From my vantage, I could look over his shoulder, and I turned to see what he was reading.

"Prayer Log," said the booklet he was browsing through. There were places to record the time, and places to record the content of the prayer. There were also occasional prompts to inspire reflective thinking. One of them read, "One thing I adore about Jesus." The young man, in his mid-twenties, wrote something down and then turned to the Latina woman sitting to his left, next to the window.

"What church do you go to?" he asked her with a smile.

The woman looked trapped, her hand moving hesitantly toward the cord one pulled to request a stop.

Ken was trying to convince me to give some Party literature to a coworker who had expressed interest in Bernie Sanders.

I thought about getting off the bus at the next stop and returning home, but I stayed on till I reached Columbia City, walking two blocks to the Hall. I pulled open the door and walked inside. There was a group meeting at a table, and Ken turned and saw me. He frowned but waved. I sat on a sofa until the group broke up about fifteen minutes later. Ken walked over to me.

"What's up?" he said.

"Thought I would come give you a ride home."

His eyebrows raised, and I handed him my spare Orca card.

"I've got the bike," he said.

"The bus has bike racks."

He nodded, and after he said good-bye to his friends, we headed across the street back to the bus stop. It being Sunday night, we had to wait almost thirty minutes before a bus came by. I helped Ken secure his bike, and we climbed aboard.

"Damn," he said. "I forgot my notebook."

"One of your friends will pick it up."

"Damn," he said again.

Two stops later, a thin white man in his mid-forties climbed up the steps. He had a deflated balloon attached to his forehead with clear Scotch tape. There were also two six-inch pieces of string taped to his cheeks, with cotton balls on the ends. Two sticks poked out of his hair. An air freshener in the shape of a Christmas tree hung from his left ear, and a large red heart cut out of construction paper was pinned to his shirt.

"Don't drive until I'm sitting down!" he ordered the driver. He then proceeded to shuffle at a snail's pace toward the back of the bus, offering cookies to any of the females he passed along the way, singing "Jingle Bells" as he went.

I looked at Ken, who was staring at the man intently.

"There's so much to do," Ken said softly. "There's so much to do."

I reached over and squeezed Ken's hand. He turned to me for a moment and then looked at the shuffling man again without saying another word.

But he squeezed my hand tightly in return.

The Gathering 16

"Wow," Jon said when Gavin was through.

"Looks like you're having second thoughts about the wonders of gay life," Nellie noted with a smile.

Gavin nodded. "Perhaps." He took a sip of his water. His purple glass was almost empty. He wished he'd stored at least one bottle of wine.

"Or maybe," said Quinn, "he just thinks even a bad gay relationship is better than living a lie."

Nellie turned to glare at Quinn and then looked at Gavin and frowned. "Is that what you really think?"

Gavin shrugged. "It's just a story."

"That's what everyone keeps saying." Nellie stabbed her runner with her needle and set it down. "Nothing is just a story." She stood up and marched to the kitchen with her yellow plastic glass.

Gavin studied the others in the room. They all looked unhappy. Perhaps all this soul searching was a bad idea. He decided he wouldn't tell any more unhappy stories. The next few days might be all they had left. There was no point in making everyone any more miserable than they had to be.

It was starting to grow dark, so Gavin lit three candles and set them up about the living room. Nellie strode back into the room so forcefully a moment later that the wind she created almost blew one of them out. There was a strange look on her face.

"What is it?" Gavin asked.

"There's no more running water," she said.

Gavin had stored about a hundred gallons. That would last a few days, maybe a few weeks if they were careful, but it wouldn't last two years. He reached over and squeezed Nellie's hand.

She looked at Gavin for a moment and then pulled her hand away and smiled brightly. She sat down and picked up her embroidery needle. "I think it's my turn to tell a story," she said. She looked at the needle in her hand for the longest time, staring at it as if she'd had a stroke and no longer knew what the object was.

Gavin frowned. Then Nellie picked up her runner and thread, wadding it all up in a bunch. She walked down the hall to the kitchen door and opened it. Gavin heard the lid of the garbage can being lifted and replaced. Nellie walked calmly back to the living room, sat down in her usual place, and began.

A House of Her Own

"Jodie Bushman, you have passed Judgment and are assigned to the top level of the Celestial Kingdom." Jesus smiled at Jodie reassuringly and motioned her gently to the side. She'd hardly been dead two days and her head was still reeling. There was a long line behind her, so she didn't ask all the questions she'd had stored up in her mind for years.

She felt a little like a small girl waiting interminably to sit on Santa's lap in Macy's. She had a mere twenty seconds to talk to the great man, and then she had to move on to let the next kid move ahead in the line. At least as a child, she only had to wait another year before her chance came to speak with Santa another twenty seconds. She wasn't sure if she'd ever have the chance to talk to Jesus again.

An officious-looking angel guided her away. "You'll take the next shuttle to Cumorah 67," he said, looking at a clipboard. "You'll meet your new husband there."

"Cumorah 67?" Jodie asked uncertainly. She looked down the hallway in the direction others were walking. Boarding a vehicle seemed a little odd. She had supposed she'd be shipped individually to her new planet in some kind of Celestial pneumatic tube.

"The name of your new planet. Where you'll live while you rule other worlds. Once you settle down, you can change the name to something you like." Kind of like a password, Jodie thought.

"My husband's been selected for me already?" she asked. She'd already seen that Steven, the man she'd been married to on Earth for forty-three years, hadn't passed Judgment. He never could give up coffee. Two of her children had passed, though, and one daughter-in-law, but the verdict was still out on all the others. The whole family had been killed just hours short of the Second Coming. So disappointing. But she was on her way to a new planet, so she supposed everything had worked out okay in the end.

"The man selected for you was a valiant spirit during the Crusades. Raped a lot fewer women than the other warriors. Really stood out." He saw the look on Jodie's face and continued quickly, "Perfect in his generation and all that, you know."

Jodie nodded. She boarded the shuttle along with about two hundred other people and secured her seat belt. It seemed odd to take off without any flight attendants giving emergency instructions. If there were to be no emergencies on Celestial flights, why were there seat belts?

"Where are you headed?" Jodie asked the woman sitting next to her.

The woman put down her scriptures, looking slightly irritated at the interruption. "Cumorah 67," she replied curtly.

"Oh, same as me." Then it dawned on her that this woman was probably going to be her sister wife. She frowned. She looked about the cabin of the aircraft. Of the two hundred passengers, maybe two-thirds were women, but there were plenty of men, too. She wondered what their destination was. She tapped the shoulder of a man in the row ahead of her. "Where are you going, sir?" she asked.

"It's Brother," he corrected. "Well, cousin, actually. Don't you remember me? We met when we were five at a family reunion. Of course, I was much older than you at the time."

"I see."

"I'm headed to Cumorah 67," the man continued.

Jodie nodded and sat back in her seat. Was everyone on this flight headed to Cumorah 67? She'd assumed that it was a multi-stop flight, everyone going to their own planet.

"Are you related to me, too?" Jodie asked the woman beside her.

The woman closed her scriptures again, sighing heavily. "We're all related. Families are forever. Didn't you pay attention in Primary?" She shook her head and returned to her book. Jodie remembered that none of them on this shuttle were perfect yet. Going to the Celestial Kingdom only meant that they were allowed to continue on the *pathway* to perfection, however long that process might eventually take.

A flight attendant walked by, and Jodie raised her hand. "Yes?" the attendant asked, smiling so that her dimples showed.

"How long is the flight?"

"Not quite six hours. We're flying fifty-four times the speed of light. We deliberately picked this speed because it gives you time to see all the orientation materials before we arrive. But don't worry, we'll be serving refreshments in just a few moments, and the meal cart will come by in a couple of hours."

"But…"

The flight attendant smiled sweetly and walked away.

Jodie unbuckled her seat belt and strained to look over the tops of the seats. There were only a handful of empty ones in the entire cabin. One of them was next to a handsome young man. Of course, everyone on board was young and beautiful, she realized, retaining just enough of their natural features to be recognizable, but clearly airbrushed in some Celestial manner. She stood up and started squeezing past the woman next to her. The woman twisted to the side and let Jodie pass with a sigh.

Jodie walked back three rows and looked at the handsome man. She wondered if the man selected for her was going to be this handsome. Since everyone was handsome, she supposed so. Steven had been a good man, and she was sorry he hadn't made it, but he'd been awful in bed, and she'd spent many a long night worrying about what his penis would look like after the resurrection. "Do you mind if I take this seat?" she asked.

"Hi, Aunt Jodie!" he said, smiling broadly.

"Aunt Jodie?" Jodie faltered. "I don't remember…"

"Oh, I died when I was a month old."

"You're Sarah's son?"

He grinned, patting the empty seat next to him. Jodie sat down, wondering if she should buckle up again. "I'm Orson. Your sister Sarah smothered me deliberately," he said. "She wanted to make sure I made it to the Celestial Kingdom." He motioned to the cabin with upturned hands. "And it worked." He shrugged. "Of course, it means she won't be here herself."

Jodie's mouth fell open.

"What a beautiful mouth. I think it'll work just perfectly."

"P-pardon me?"

"I'm your new husband. I was hoping you'd feel the Spirit and move over next to me." He offered his hand.

"But you're my nephew." Jodie started to offer her hand but couldn't decide if she should do so or not and finally withdrew it.

"Families are forever," said Orson with a smile.

"I was told my new husband had lived during the Crusades." She frowned.

"Oh, that. It's true enough. I sinned a lot technically my first go around, but I was so much better than everyone else at the time they let me come back into a Mormon family." He grinned. "But I've still got a little of that Crusader in me." He looked at her breasts, and Jodie realized they were a lot perkier than they'd been the last few decades. They were also larger than they'd been when she was alive. She instinctively touched them. Orson's grin was a little toothier now.

"But Mormons don't believe in reincarnation," Jodie said, getting back to the point at hand.

"Believing or not believing something doesn't make a thing so. And it was only those who were borderline who were given a second chance. Most people aren't borderline."

Jodie nodded hesitantly at the new doctrine, rubbing her chin. Then she had another thought and looked about the cabin again, more slowly this time. "Is everyone on this flight related to us?"

Orson laughed. "Well, of course they are. Everyone on our entire planet will be related to us. And they try to group the more closely related people on any one shuttle."

Jodie looked at him and frowned. "How many people will there be on our planet?" she asked.

"We won't know for sure until Judgment is over for everyone, and that'll take some time. But of course you'll want any of your kids and grandkids who make it to the top kingdom to still be with you, won't you? That was pretty much the Church's main focus, wasn't it?"

"Yes," Jodie admitted, "but…"

"Not that I ever got to go to church on Earth," he continued. "But we had Primary and Sacrament meeting in the Spirit World, too, you know. Those are eternal classes. We'll have them on Cumorah 67, too."

Oh, dear, thought Jodie. She leaned forward to look past Orson and out the window. Everything was black. If there were stars, they were too faint to be seen against the lights coming from overhead flooding the cabin.

"So of course our immediate families will be there with us," Orson continued. "And our siblings and our parents. And our parents' siblings, and our cousins' immediate families and grandkids. And our grandparents' siblings and their families. And of course, our grandparents wouldn't be happy in the Celestial Kingdom if they were separated from *their* parents. Because, you know…"

"Families are forever."

Orson smiled.

Jodie rubbed her chin and fiddled with the magazine in the pocket on the back of the seat in front of her. It was a copy of the *Liahona*. She pulled it out and flipped through it, but she didn't understand the language. She'd have all eternity to learn every language she wanted. She put the magazine back.

"So how far back does this go?" Jodie asked carefully.

Orson laughed. "I swear, Aunt Jodie, I don't know how you passed Judgment. You sure don't seem to have paid attention very well to the prophets."

"Well, I was always a very good girl," Jodie said defensively. "I always just did what I was told."

Orson nodded appreciatively. "That seems to have done the trick." He grinned again. "I can't wait till we're married." Orson looked down at her knees and then back at her.

Jodie smiled uncertainly. "So to answer my question?" she persisted.

Orson waved as if swatting casually at a fly. "Aunt Jodie, *everyone* will be there. Anyone who goes to the Celestial

Kingdom. If someone wasn't there, *someone* would be without a family member. And that was the contract, after all—if we were obedient, we'd be with our families forever."

"But…but…"

Orson sighed, sounding now like the woman from the other seat. "Aunt Jodie, I hope you aren't going to keep this up for eternity." He paused and looked at his open hand. "Can I still call you Aunt Jodie after we're married?"

Jodie ignored the question and asked one of her own. "Just how big is Cumorah 67?" she asked. "Won't you and I…" She swallowed. "…have billions of spirit children of our own? Won't they all be there, too, until they go off to whatever planet we create for their test?"

"Sure," Orson said with a look of confusion. "I don't understand the question. *Everyone* on Cumorah 67 will have billions of spirit children. They'll all be with us, because they're all family. Cumorah 67 is ten times the size of Jupiter. There'll be plenty of room. Am I misunderstanding your question?"

Jodie turned away and looked about the cabin again. Then Orson lifted her hand and placed it on his knee with a smile. She withdrew it into her lap. "Why is it called Cumorah 67 if everyone is going to the same place?" she asked. "If no one's going to any other Cumorahs?"

"I guess because it sounds cool." Orson shrugged. "Though there's no reason we can't rename it Cumorah 69." He ran his tongue along his top lip.

The lights dimmed, and Orson nudged Jodie. "Get your ear buds ready. The movie's about to begin."

Jodie inserted the ear buds and watched as the screen descended over the back of the seat in front of her. "Welcome to the Celestial Kingdom," a baritone voice said pleasantly as a photo of a beam of light breaking through cumulus clouds came onto the screen. "Here's what you need to know to make Day One a success."

Jodie looked about the cabin again, her eyes focusing on the pressurized door. She wondered if there was any way to open it mid-flight.

A man in a white robe appeared on screen, but Jodie was barely listening. She was thinking back on how she'd grown up in a family of eight children, had married a man and borne six children of her own. She'd always been her parents' daughter, her husband's wife, her children's mother, her grandchildren's grandmother.

And now she was going to be with a family of trillions.

When did she get a house of her own?

She looked again at the cabin door and started unbuckling her seat belt. Just then, a flight attendant pulled her cart alongside Jodie's row. "Beverage?" she asked with a white, toothy smile but no dimples. "We have coffee now. And wine," she added with a twinkle.

"How about whiskey?" asked Jodie heavily.

The flight attendant smiled and nodded.

"Then make it a double."

The flight attendant handed her a glass and Jodie took a long sip. Orson put his hand on her knee and squeezed. She sighed and turned back to the screen in front of her. A handsome angel was talking with a melodious voice.

Jodie took another sip.

The Gathering 17

When Nellie finished speaking, Gavin looked about at all the others in the room. They had expressions of pity mixed with sadness and embarrassment, the same emotions twisting painfully inside Gavin's soul, no matter how blank his face might be. "Nellie," he said softly, "why did you tell a story like that? Just because we're all doubting doesn't mean we want you to."

But what else had he expected? Nellie was only human. She could be worn down just like anyone else. Just as he'd been over the past thirty or forty years. Somehow, he had thought she was invincible. It was one of the reasons he'd married her, to be strong for him. Be valiant for him by proxy.

Just as he had stayed true to her, as if that would bring him love by proxy.

"I feel better when I'm being contrary," said Quinn, "but Gavin's right. We still need *someone* to be strong."

Nellie shook her head. She walked over to the figurine of the woman and two children sitting on top of the bookcase, examined it a moment, and set it down in disgust. Even in the dim light of the flickering candles, Gavin could read her expression. "The past week has made me think about a lot of things," she said. "And these past couple of days listening to all of you. I…I'm afraid I may have been mistaken."

"No…" said Emma soothingly.

"No…" said Jon.

Quinn didn't say anything. And Gavin didn't know what to say, either. They could hear shouting off in the distance somewhere down the block. Why didn't God make all the mean people die of the plague? What was the point of only killing off *half* the bad people? If the ratio of good to bad was the same as before the calamities, what difference did surviving to the Last Days make?

"We're the elect," said Nellie, "and look how awful we are. Even a god isn't powerful enough to save humanity."

A dog started barking incessantly outside. There was a sudden squeal and it stopped. It was still early yet, not even 8:00, but perhaps they ought to stop telling stories and go to their rooms. Even if there was no peace inside their own heads, sleep might offer them a respite.

"This is the greatest trial anyone's ever had to face," Gavin finally managed. "Because it comes right before the greatest event in two thousand years. In some ways, it's the most important event in the history of the planet. It's *supposed* to be hard. We're all just a little tired, that's all. You'll feel better in the morning, Nellie. We all will."

The baby murmured, and Quinn kneeled beside her and caressed her head.

"I'm sorry to bring you all down," Nellie replied. "But pretending to be strong all these years isn't the same thing as really *being* strong."

"You *are* strong, honey. I'd never have made it this far in life without you." He paused and decided to add something he no longer believed. "You're my savior."

She didn't say anything in return, just looked at him and nodded slowly.

They listened as the sound of shouting grew louder outside in the darkness. They heard glass break at the house next door. Jon moved closer to Emma on the sofa.

"It'll be us sooner or later," Nellie said in a monotone.

"Heavenly Father will protect us," said Emma. "Just as he always has." Her brows furrowed and she looked at her wedding ring. "We'll all see the face of Jesus soon." She turned now to Jon. "Soon, we'll…" she began but seemed to lose her train of thought. "Soon…"

Nellie looked at Gavin with the most naked expression he'd ever seen. He didn't have the heart to lie any more. "Do you think," he said slowly, "that maybe there's no Second Coming?"

He looked about at the others, and they seemed as devastated as he felt at hearing the words finally spoken aloud. "Maybe we just fucked up the world, thinking someone else was going to come along and magically fix everything. When really it was up to us all along."

Nellie stood up and walked over to Gavin's recliner. She sat down on his lap and rested her head on his shoulder. "You've suffered so much," she said. "I'm truly sorry."

Gavin's throat closed and he couldn't speak. He wanted to tell her he loved her. But even now, he wasn't sure he did.

There was more shouting outside, and Jon squeezed Emma's hand. Quinn was looking down at the baby and crying.

I want another chance! Gavin thought desperately. He looked at the tiny flames stationed about the room, giving off so little light.

"Where's the gun?" Emma whispered, turning toward the ficus tree.

"What's the use?" Jon answered.

"Oh, Eric, I wish you were here."

Something crashed through the window, and the rush of air blew out the candles. Nellie never saw the expression on Gavin's face as he held her tightly in the dark and waited calmly for what was to come.

Books by Johnny Townsend

Mormon Underwear

God's Gargoyles

The Circumcision of God

Sex among the Saints

Dinosaur Perversions

Zombies for Jesus

A Gay Mormon Missionary in Pompeii

The Gay Mormon Quilter's Club

The Golem of Rabbi Loew

Mormon Fairy Tales

Flying over Babel

Marginal Mormons

Mormon Bullies

The Mormon Victorian Society

Dragons of the Book of Mormon

Selling the City of Enoch

A Day at the Temple

Behind the Zion Curtain

Gayrabian Nights

Lying for the Lord

Despots of Deseret

Missionaries Make the Best Companions

Invasion of the Spirit Snatchers

The Tyranny of Silence

Sex on the Sabbath

The Washing of Brains

The Mormon Inquisition

Interview with a Mission President

Weeping, Wailing, and Gnashing of Teeth

Behind the Bishop's Door

The Moat around Zion

The Last Days Linger

Mormon Madness

Human Compassion for Beginners

Dead Mankind Walking

Breaking the Promise of the Promised Land

Am I My Planet's Keeper?

Have Your Cum and Eat It, Too

Strangers with Benefits

Constructing Equity

Wake Up and Smell the Missionaries

Racism by Proxy

Orgy at the STD Clinic

Please Evacuate

Recommended Daily Humanity

The Camper Killings

An Eternity of Mirrors: Best Short Stories of Johnny Townsend

Inferno in the French Quarter: The UpStairs Lounge Fire

Latter-Gay Saints: An Anthology of Gay Mormon Fiction (co-editor)

Available from your favorite neighborhood or online bookstore.

Wondering what some of those other books are about? Read on!

Gayrabian Nights

Gayrabian Nights is a twist on the well-known classic, *1001 Arabian Nights*, in which Scheherazade, under the threat of death if she ceases to captivate King Shahryar's attention, enchants him through a series of mysterious, adventurous, and romantic tales.

In this variation, a male escort, invited to the hotel room of a closeted, homophobic Mormon senator, learns that the man is poised to vote on a piece of anti-gay legislation the following morning. To prevent him from sleeping, so that the exhausted senator will miss casting his vote on the Senate floor, the escort entertains him with stories of homophobia, celibacy, mixed orientation marriages, reparative therapy, coming out, first love, gay marriage, and long-term successful gay relationships. The escort crafts the stories to give the senator a crash course in gay culture and sensibilities, hoping to bring the man closer to accepting his own sexual orientation.

Inferno in the French Quarter: The UpStairs Lounge Fire

On Gay Pride Day in 1973, someone set the entrance to a French Quarter gay bar on fire. In the terrible inferno that followed, thirty-two people lost their lives, including a third of the local congregation of the Metropolitan Community Church, their pastor burning to death halfway out a second-story window as he tried to claw his way to freedom. A mother who'd gone to the bar with her two gay sons died alongside them. A man who'd helped his friend escape first was found dead near the fire escape. Two children waited outside a movie theater across town for a father and step-father who would never pick them up. During this era of rampant homophobia, several families refused to claim the bodies, and many churches refused to bury the dead. Author Johnny Townsend pored through old records and tracked down survivors of the fire as well as relatives and friends of those killed to compile this fascinating account of a forgotten moment in gay history.

A Gay Mormon Missionary in Pompeii

What is a gay Mormon missionary doing in Italy? He is trying to save his own soul as well as the souls of others. In these tales chronicling the two-year mission of Robert Anderson, we see a young man tormented by his inability to be the man the Church says he should be. In addition to his personal hell, Anderson faces a major earthquake, organized crime, a serious bus accident, and much more. He copes with horrendous mission leaders and his own suicidal tendencies. But one day, he meets another missionary who loves him, and his world changes forever.

Missionaries Make the Best Companions

What lies behind the freshly scrubbed façades of the Mormon missionaries we see about town? In these stories, an ex-Mormon tries to seduce a faithful elder by showing him increasingly suggestive movies. A sister missionary fulfills her community service requirement by babysitting for a prostitute. Two elders break their mission rules by venturing into the forbidden French Quarter. A senior missionary couple try to reactivate lapsed members while their own family falls apart back home. A young man hopes that serving a second full-time mission will lead him up the Church hierarchy. Two bored missionaries decide to make a little extra money moonlighting in a male stripper club. Two frustrated elders find an acceptable way to masturbate—by donating to a Fertility Clinic. A lonely man searches for the favorite companion he hasn't seen in thirty years.

The Golem of Rabbi Loew

Jacob and Esau Cohen are the closest of brothers. In fact, they're lovers. A doctor tries to combine canine genes with those of Jews, to improve their chances of surviving a hostile world. A Talmudic scholar dates an escort. A scientist tries to develop the "God spot" in the brains of his patients in order to create a messiah. The Golem of Prague is really Rabbi Loew's secret lover. While some of the Jews in Townsend's book are Orthodox, this collection of Jewish stories most certainly is not.

The Last Days Linger

The scriptures tell us that in the Last Days, wickedness will increase upon the Earth. When leaders of the Mormon Church see a rise in the number of gay members, they believe the end is upon them. But while "wickedness never was happiness," it begins to appear that wickedness can sometimes be divine. At least, the stories here suggest that religious proscriptions condemning homosexuality have it all wrong. While gay Mormons may be no closer to perfection than anyone else, they're no further from it, either. And sometimes, being gay provides just the right ingredient to create saints—as flawed as God himself.

Mormon Madness

Mental illness can strike the faithful as easily as anyone else. But often religious doctrine and practice exacerbate rather than alleviate these problems. From schizophrenia to obsessive-compulsive disorder, from persecution complex to sexual dysfunction, autism to dissociative identity disorder, Mormons must cope with their mental as well as their spiritual health on a daily basis.

Am I My Planet's Keeper?

Global Warming. Climate Change. Climate Crisis. Climate Emergency. Whatever label we use, we are facing one of the greatest challenges to the survival of life as we know it.

But while addressing greenhouse gases is perhaps our most urgent need, it's not our only task. We must also address toxic waste, pollution, habitat destruction, and our other contributions to the world's sixth mass extinction event.

In order to do that, we must simultaneously address the unmet human needs that keep us distracted from deeper engagement in stabilizing our climate: moderating economic inequality, guaranteeing healthcare to all, and ensuring education for everyone.

And to accomplish *that*, we must unite to combat the monied forces that use fear, prejudice, and misinformation to manipulate us.

It's a daunting task. But success is our only option.

Wake Up and Smell the Missionaries

Two Mormon missionaries in Italy discover they share the same rare ability—both can emit pheromones on demand. At first, they playfully compete in the hills of Frascati to see who can tempt "investigators" most. But soon they're targeting each other non-stop.

Can two immature young men learn to control their "superpower" to live a normal life…and develop genuine love? Even as their relationship is threatened by the attentions of another man?

They seem just on the verge of success when a massive earthquake leaves them trapped under the rubble of their apartment in Castellammare.

With night falling and temperatures dropping, can they dig themselves out in time to save themselves? And will their injuries destroy the ability that brought them together in the first place?

Orgy at the STD Clinic

Todd Tillotson is struggling to move on after his husband is killed in a hit and run attack a year earlier during a Black Lives Matter protest in Seattle.

In this novel set entirely on public transportation, we watch as Todd, isolated throughout the pandemic, battles desperation in his attempt to safely reconnect with the world.

Will he find love again, even casual friendship, or will he simply end up another crazy old man on the bus?

Things don't look good until a man whose face he can't even see sits down beside him despite the raging variants.

And asks him a question that will change his life.

Please Evacuate

A gay, partygoing New Yorker unconcerned about the future or the unsustainability of capitalism is hit by a truck and thrust into a straight man's body half a continent away. As Hunter tries to figure out what's happening, he's caught up in another disaster, a wildfire sweeping through a Colorado community, the flames overtaking him and several schoolchildren as they flee.

When he awakens, Hunter finds himself in the body of yet another man, this time in northern Italy, a former missionary about to marry a young Mormon woman. Still piecing together this new reality, and beginning to embrace his latest identity, Hunter fights for his life in a devastating flash flood along with his wife *and* his new husband.

He's an aging worker in drought-stricken Texas, a nurse at an assisted living facility in the direct path of a hurricane, an advocate for the unhoused during a freak Seattle blizzard.

We watch as Hunter is plunged into life after life, finally recognizing the futility of only looking out for #1 and understanding the part he must play in addressing the global climate crisis...if he ever gets another chance.

Recommended Daily Humanity

A checklist of human rights must include basic housing, universal healthcare, equitable funding for public schools, and tuition-free college and vocational training.

In addition to the basics, though, we need much more to fully thrive. Subsidized childcare, universal pre-K, a universal basic income, subsidized high-speed internet, net neutrality, fare-free public transit (plus *more* public transit), and medically assisted death for the terminally ill who want it.

None of this will matter, though, if we neglect to address the rapidly worsening climate crisis.

Sound expensive? It is.

But not as expensive as refusing to implement these changes. The cost of climate disasters each year has grown to staggering figures. And the cost of social and political upheaval from not meeting the needs of suffering workers, families, and individuals may surpass even that.

It's best we understand that the vast sums required to enact meaningful change are an investment which will pay off not only in some indeterminate future but in fact almost immediately. And without these adjustments to our lifestyles and values, there may very well not be a future capable of sustaining freedom and democracy…or even civilization itself.

The Camper Killings

When a homeless man is found murdered a few blocks from Morgan Beylerian's house in south Seattle, everyone seems to consider the body just so much additional trash to be cleared from the neighborhood. But Morgan liked the guy. They used to chat when Morgan brought Nick groceries once a week.

And the brutal way the man was killed reminds Morgan of their shared Mormon heritage, back when the faithful agreed to have their throats slit if they ever revealed temple secrets.

Did Nick's former wife take action when her ex-husband refused to grant a temple divorce? Did his murder have something to do with the public accusations that brought an end to his promising career?

Morgan does his best to investigate when no one else seems to care, but it isn't easy as a man living paycheck to paycheck himself, only able to pursue his investigation via public transit.

As he continues his search for the killer, Morgan's friends withdraw and his husband threatens to leave. When another homeless man is killed and Morgan is accused of the crime, things look even bleaker.

But his troubles aren't over yet.

Will Morgan find the killer before the killer finds him?

What Readers Have Said

Townsend's stories are "a gay *Portnoy's Complaint* of Mormonism. Salacious, sweet, sad, insightful, insulting, religiously ethnic, quirky-faithful, and funny."

D. Michael Quinn, author of *The Mormon Hierarchy: Origins of Power*

"Told from a believably conversational first-person perspective, [*A Gay Mormon Missionary in Pompeii*'s] novelistic focus on Anderson's journey to thoughtful self-acceptance allows for greater character development than often seen in short stories, which makes this well-paced work rich and satisfying, and one of Townsend's strongest. An extremely important contribution to the field of Mormon fiction." Named to Kirkus Reviews' Best of 2011.

Kirkus Reviews

"The thirteen stories in *Mormon Underwear* capture this struggle [between Mormonism and homosexuality] with humor, sadness, insight, and sometimes shocking details....*Mormon Underwear* provides compelling stories, literally from the inside-out."

Niki D'Andrea, *Phoenix New Times*

"Townsend's lively writing style and engaging characters [in *Zombies for Jesus*] make for stories which force us to wake up, smell the (prohibited) coffee, and review our attitudes with regard to reading dogma so doggedly. These are tales which revel in the individual tics and quirks which make us human, Mormon or not, gay or not…"

A.J. Kirby, *The Short Review*

"The Rift," from *A Gay Mormon Missionary in Pompeii*, is a "fascinating tale of an untenable situation…a *tour de force*."

David Lenson, editor, *The Massachusetts Review*

"Pronouncing the Apostrophe," from *The Golem of Rabbi Loew*, is "quiet and revealing, an intriguing tale…"

Sima Rabinowitz, Literary Magazine Review, *NewPages.com*

The Circumcision of God is "a collection of short stories that consider the imperfect, silenced majority of Mormons, who may in fact be [the Church's] best hope….[The book leaves] readers regretting the church's willingness to marginalize those who best exemplify its ideals: those who love fiercely despite all obstacles, who brave challenges at great personal risk and who always choose the hard, higher road."

Kirkus Reviews

In *Mormon Fairy Tales*, Johnny Townsend displays "both a wicked sense of irony and a deep well of compassion."

Kel Munger, *Sacramento News and Review*

Zombies for Jesus is "eerie, erotic, and magical."

Publishers Weekly

"While [Townsend's] many touching vignettes draw deeply from Mormon mythology, history, spirituality and culture, [*Mormon Fairy Tales*] is neither a gaudy act of proselytism nor angry protest literature from an ex-believer. Like all good fiction, his stories are simply about the joys, the hopes and the sorrows of people."

Kirkus Reviews

"In *Inferno in the French Quarter* author Johnny Townsend restores this tragic event [the UpStairs Lounge fire] to its proper place in LGBT history and reminds us that the victims of the blaze
were not just 'statistics,' but real people with real lives, families, and friends."

Jesse Monteagudo, *The Bilerico Project*

In *Inferno in the French Quarter*, "Townsend's heart-rending descriptions of the victims…seem to [make them] come alive once more."

Kit Van Cleave, *OutSmart Magazine*

Marginal Mormons is "an irreverent, honest look at life outside the mainstream Mormon Church….Throughout his musings on sin and forgiveness, Townsend beautifully demonstrates his characters' internal, perhaps irreconcilable struggles….Rather than anger and disdain, he offers an honest portrayal of people searching for meaning and community in their lives, regardless of their life choices or secrets." Named to Kirkus Reviews' Best of 2012.

Kirkus Reviews

The stories in *The Mormon Victorian Society* "register the new openness and confidence of gay life in the age of same-sex marriage….What hasn't changed is Townsend's wry, conversational prose, his subtle evocations of character and social dynamics, and his deadpan humor. His warm empathy still glows in this intimate yet clear-eyed engagement with Mormon theology and folkways. Funny, shrewd and finely wrought dissections of the awkward contradictions—and surprising harmonies—between conscience and desire." Named to Kirkus Reviews' Best of 2013.

Kirkus Reviews

"This collection of short stories [*The Mormon Victorian Society*] featuring gay Mormon characters slammed [me] in the face from the first page, wrestled my heart and mind to the floor, and left me panting and wanting more by the end. Johnny Townsend has created so many memorable characters in such few pages. I went weeks thinking about this book. It truly touched me."

Tom Webb, *A Bear on Books*

Dragons of the Book of Mormon is an "entertaining collection….Townsend's prose is sharp, clear, and easy to read, and his characters are well rendered…"

Publishers Weekly

"The pre-eminent documenter of alternative Mormon lifestyles…Townsend has a deep understanding of his characters, and his limpid prose, dry humor and well-grounded (occasionally magical) realism make their spiritual conundrums both compelling and entertaining. [*Dragons of the Book of Mormon* is] [a]nother of Townsend's critical but affectionate and absorbing tours of Mormon discontent." Named to Kirkus Reviews' Best of 2014.

Kirkus Reviews

Gayrabian Nights "was easily the most original book I've read all year. Funny, touching, topical, and thoroughly enjoyable."

Rainbow Awards

In *Gayrabian Nights*, "Townsend's prose is always limpid and evocative, and…he finds real drama and emotional depth in the most ordinary of lives."

Kirkus Reviews

Lying for the Lord is "one of the most gripping books that I've picked up for quite a while. I love the author's writing style, alternately cynical, humorous, biting, scathing, poignant, and touching…. This is the third book of his that I've read, and all are equally engaging. These are stories that need to be told, and the author does it in just the right way."

Heidi Alsop, *Ex-Mormon Foundation Board Member*

In *Lying for the Lord*, Townsend "gets under the skin of his characters to reveal their complexity and conflicts….shrewd, evocative [and] wryly humorous."

Kirkus Reviews

In *Missionaries Make the Best Companions*, "the author treats the clash between religious dogma and liberal humanism with vivid realism, sly humor, and subtle feeling as his characters try to figure out their true missions in life. Another of Townsend's rich dissections of Mormon failures and uncertainties…" Named to Kirkus Reviews' Best of 2015.

Kirkus Reviews

The Washing of Brains has "A lovely writing style, and each story [is] full of unique, engaging characters....immensely entertaining."

Rainbow Awards

"Townsend's collection [*The Washing of Brains*] once again displays his limpid, naturalistic prose, skillful narrative chops, and his subtle insights into psychology…Well-crafted dispatches on the clash between religion and self-fulfillment…"

Kirkus Reviews

"Johnny Townsend's 'Partying with St. Roch' [in the anthology *Latter-Gay Saints*] tells a beautiful, haunting tale."

Kent Brintnall, Out in Print: Queer Book Reviews

"While the author is generally at his best when working as a satirist, there are some fine, understated touches in these tales [*The Last Days Linger*] that will likely affect readers in subtle ways….readers should come away impressed by the deep empathy he shows for all his characters—even the homophobic ones."

Kirkus Reviews

"Written in a conversational style that often uses stories and personal anecdotes to reveal larger truths, this immensely approachable book [*Racism by Proxy*] skillfully serves its intended audience of White readers grappling with complex questions regarding race, history, and identity. The author's frequent references to the Church of Jesus Christ of Latter-day Saints may be too niche for readers unfamiliar with its idiosyncrasies, but Townsend generally strikes a perfect balance of humor, introspection, and reasoned arguments that will engage even skeptical readers."

Kirkus Reviews

Orgy at the STD Clinic portrays "an all-too real scenario that Townsend skewers to wincingly accurate proportions…[with] instant classic moments courtesy of his punchy, sassy, sexy lead character…"

Jim Piechota, *Bay Area Reporter*

Orgy at the STD Clinic is "…a triumph of humane sensibility. A richly textured saga that brilliantly captures the fraying social fabric of contemporary life." Named to Kirkus Reviews' Best Indie Books of 2022.

Kirkus Reviews

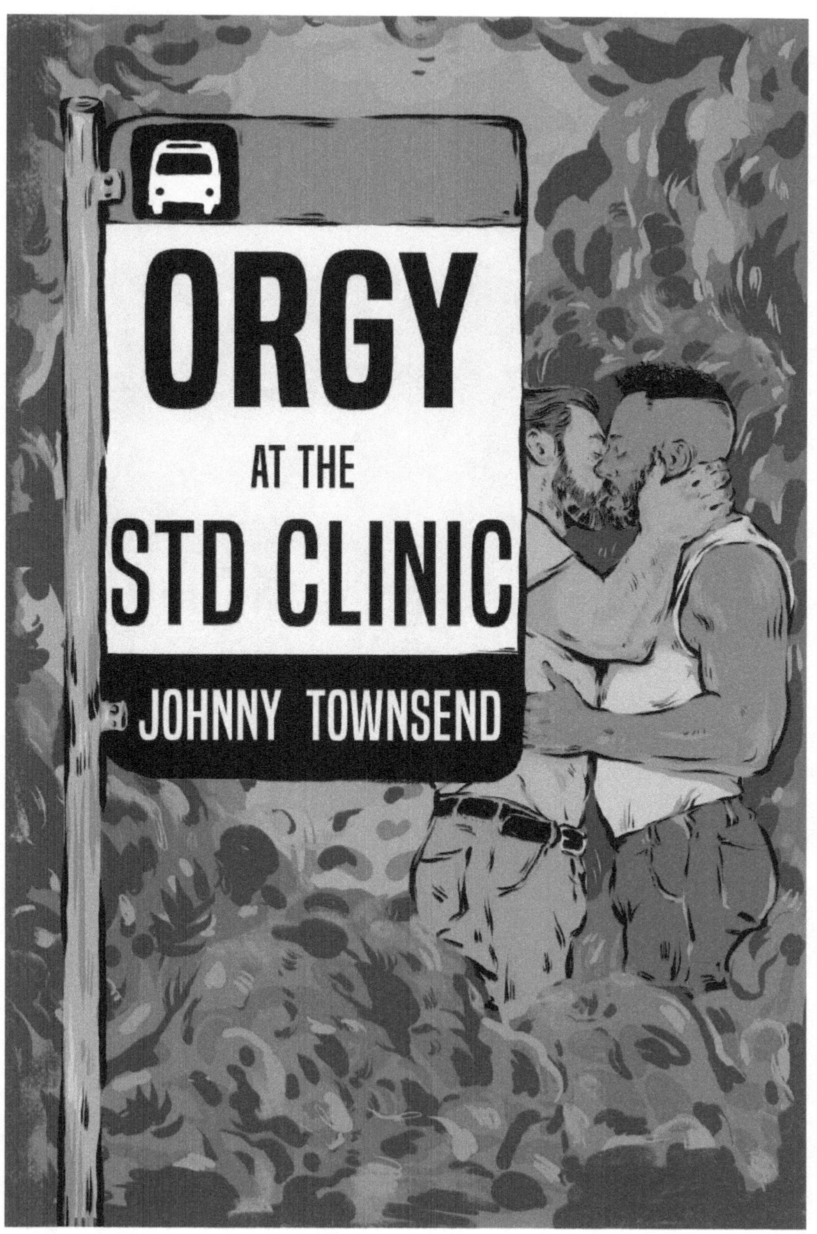
ORGY
AT THE
STD CLINIC
JOHNNY TOWNSEND

HAVE
YOUR CUM
AND
EAT IT, TOO
JOHNNY TOWNSEND